Alexander Anderson

A song of labour and other poems

Alexander Anderson

A song of labour and other poems

ISBN/EAN: 9783744722322

Printed in Europe, USA, Canada, Australia, Japan

Cover: Foto ©Andreas Hilbeck / pixelio.de

More available books at **www.hansebooks.com**

A SONG OF LABOUR

AND

OTHER POEMS.

BY

ALEXANDER ANDERSON,

(RAILWAY SURFACEMAN.)

KIRKCONNEL, VIA SANQUHAR, DUMFRIESSHIRE.

DUNDEE:

PRINTED AT THE ADVERTISER OFFICE, BANK STREET.

1873.

PREFACE.

SOME time ago a wish was kindly expressed by several of my friends, and others who had read my verses as they appeared in print, that I should publish them in a collected form. The idea of having a book of my own, I admit, was not easily got rid of, so, after a little deliberation and reflection, I determined to venture into the realms of authorship. Such an undertaking is, in these times, rather hazardous for an unknown author to engage in ; but still I had the hope, in common with other warblers, that there might be room enough left to pipe what little song there was in me. In this hope the present adventure is made ; and the result, for better or worse, is now beyond the control of the Author and in the hands of the Public, whose verdict I now submissively await.

The Poems in this collection have, for the most part, already appeared in the pages of the *People's Friend*, under the *nom-de-plume* "Surfaceman ;" and I think it but just to myself to state that this title truly designates the nature of my calling—I being but a humble son of toil, working with pick and shovel on the railway. Other Poems, which appeared in several of the London Magazines, are, by the kind permission of the Publishers, inserted in the volume; and these, with a considerable number of others which have never appeared in print before, constitute the collection which I now offer to the Public, in the hope that, as I have had great delight in the writing of them, the reader may have—though in a less degree—a pleasure in their perusal.

I leave the Poems, then, to those who, like **myself, have to toil for their daily bread; and** if my verses influence them in the slightest degree towards a higher reverence for the "nobility **of** labour, the **long** pedigree of toil," I shall tear the account which, more **or less, stands** between the author and his readers, **and, like** the gnome in the German story, fling it in their faces with these two words written upon it—"Fully paid."

I cannot conclude without touching upon a duty which is heavier than I at first had imagined—I mean the tendering of my thanks to all my friends, far and near, who generously came forward to aid **me in** the launch **of my little book.** I have no set words in which to couch my gratitude to them. I can only request them to fancy what, in my inability to express, I have **left unsaid.**

CONTENTS.

CONTENTS.

POEMS.

A SONG OF LABOUR.

RESPECTFULLY DEDICATED TO MY FELLOW-WORKERS WITH PICK AND SHOVEL
EVERYWHERE.

"Let each man honour his workmanship—his Can-do."—CARLYLE.

LET us sing, my toiling Brothers, with our rough, rude voice a
  song
 That shall live behind, nor do us in the after ages wrong,
But forever throb and whisper strength to nerve our fellow kind
As they rise to fill our footsteps and the space we leave behind.
What though hand and form be rugged? better then for Labour's
  mart—
I have never heard that Nature changed the colour of the heart—
The God above hath made us one in flesh and blood with kings,
But the lower use is ours, and all the force of rougher things.
Then, my Brothers, sing to Labour, as the sun-brown'd giant stands
Like an Atlas with the world shaking in his mighty hands;
Brawny arm'd, and broad, and swarthy, keeping in with shout and
  groan,
In the arch of life the keystone that the world may thunder on;
Ever toiling, ever sweating, ever knowing that to day
Is the footstool for the coming years to reach a higher sway.

A

Up, then, we, his rugged children, as the big hours move and pant,
For that cannot be but noble what he claims and cannot want :
Sing, and let his myriad voices bear the burden far along,
While we hail the mighty engine as the spirit of our song !

Arm to arm, and let the metals into proper range be thrown,
Let us smooth the iron pathway to the monster coming on.
Lo ! he dawns adown the distance, and his iron footway rings
As he bounds, a wander'd meteor, muffled up in smoky wings—
Earth beneath his mighty footsteps trembles at the sudden load,
As of old the field Scamander at the falling of the god.
Give him freedom, strength he needs not, only space and bound to
      fly,
As at night, in starry silence, glides a planet through the sky—
Thus he comes, the earth-born splendour, and with sudden shriek
      and gasp
On he flames, the Jove of Commerce, with the lightnings in his
      grasp.
O, my Brothers, this is something, in the fret and rush of days,
Worthy of our love and wonder, and the throbbing out of praise ;
Then another wilder pæan for this march of thought and mind,
Some ecstatic dithyrambus that shall deify our kind.

Arm to arm, and let the metals into proper range be thrown,
Let us shape the iron pathway for the monster coming on ,
Make his footing sure and steady, fitting for a thing like him,
Rolling out his seven-leagued paces smoother than a bird can skim ;
Drawing city unto city, flinging with his grasp of steel
Nations into shape and method, till his muscles shake and reel ;
Stretching outward, like Briareus, hundred arms of sudden stroke,
Shooting upward to the heavens coiling Laöcoons of smoke ;
Touching, like the gods of fable, all things into noble strife
As before the heated sculptor flash'd the statue into life.
O, what strength shall be his portion in the coming reach of time,
When his sinews swell and ripen into firm and perfect prime,
He shall be the untired monster that like Gulliver shall lead
Busy peoples to each other only with an iron thread.

Heart ! but this old world rolls onward through the shadows of the
      years,
Swift as fell the reckless Phæton headlong through the startled
      spheres ;

And along with it we struggle, shaping bounds we slowly reach,
For this knowledge is a master whose first aim is to unteach.
So, he moves with time and patience, working with a careful heed,
Growing more and more in earnest when he moulds the perfect
    deed ;
Therefore guide him well, and listen to his slightest spoken word,
For a simple note will sometimes lead us to a fuller chord ;
And the finish'd triumph with us shall a hundredfold repay
All the toil, and search, and panting for the source of purer day.
" But," says one who still will murmur in the camp of brother-
    hood,
" Progress comes with tardy footsteps, and can do the grave no
    · good."
There but spoke the Cynic, Brothers, curbing down with strongest
    steel
All the width of human purpose, all that brain can do and feel ;
Scorning ever outward action, but to wrap himself in toils
Spun to catch the things that wither, spun to catch the dust that
    soils.
Shame on such ! they are not worthy of the common breath they
    draw,
Since with it they make existence wither to a narrow law.
Wider range and freer action, nobler maxims for my breath ;
I would wish my fellows success from the very jaws of death :
Death ! a moment's cunning darkness flung across the trembling
    eyes
As we flash into the spirit cradled in a wild surprise.
Then what motions come upon us, golden laws of sudden calm,
Raining down eternal silence, raining down eternal balm.
Dare I fix my vision further, deeming that we mould this mind,
But to look in steady splendour on the toiling of our kind ?
Heart ! but this were something nobler than the poet ever felt
When the fought-for happy laurel clasp'd his forehead like a belt ;
When the liquid fire of genius, rainbow colour'd, flash'd and
    glow'd
All its mighty beams above him with the splendour of a god :
Wilder in its stretch and grandeur than the brain could ever dream
To look down upon our fellows from some planet's blinding gleam,
Watching with seraphic vision, grasping with delighted soul
All the goals to which they hurry as the moments shake and roll,
Linking with an unseen quickness vigour to the tasks they do,
Touching each with new impulses as a nobler comes in view.

Then when triumph crowns their striving, start to hear the heavens
    sublime,
Fill its azure arch with plaudits rushing from the throat of time ;
And to hear the poets singing far above the rush of feet
Epithalamiums of madness when the links of success meet.
This is frenzy, and the overstretching of unhealthy strings,
Let us touch a chord that trembles to the breath of higher things.
Rash in him who sings unworthy, looking not within his heart
For the counsel that should guide him to the honours of his art.
"Sing you thus?" I hear you question, and I answer you again,
I but fit me to that measure chance flings blindly down on men,
Which requires nor heart nor passion, but the will that makes a
    voice—
Mighty poets sing by impulse, and the lesser but by choice.
"Yet you claim the meed of poet?" and I answer firm and strong,
Count me only as a poet, Brothers, while I sing this song.

Arm to arm, and let the metals into proper range be thrown,
Let us shape the iron pathway for the monster coming on.
What though we be feeble puppets with a little vigour crown'd,
Yet this task is ours, to fence his footsteps into proper bound ;
Therefore guide him well, nor tamper with the thread that leads his
    powers,
Since the splendour of his mission flings a dignity on ours.

As the silent sage at midnight shapes his cunning thoughts to
    smoothe
Pathways through the world's jungle for the steady tramp of
    truth ;
As the pioneer that fells the sounding forest tree by tree,
With a mighty thought that trembles to the settlement to be ;
As the sentinel who slowly paces as the night hours fly,
With the lives of breathing thousands hanging on his watchful
    eye ;
As within the field of Sempach in the bleeding Swiss's breast
Freedom found her purple dwelling, giving to a nation rest ;
As the coral insect toiling in the ocean's mighty vast
Rears a giant's labour upward through the swaying surge at last ;
So the specks that dot existence, seeming blind and aimless still,
Knit in one, are levers waiting for the touch of thought and will.
Thus are we but toiling units, rough at heart and brown in face,
Noble only to be useful, lowly in a lowly place ;

Filling up the ruts existence furrows with his heavy wain,
That the nobler hearts behind may start and sow the fruitful
    grain ;
For we clothe with tougher muscle circles of a mighty whole,
Moving at the touch of fellows with a greater breadth of soul.
But I crave not higher mission than to shape the ends they think,
Deeming I am all but godlike in the holding of a link.
And this link for ever widens, as their restless spirits teach,
Till it forms a chain of union clanking from the heart of each ;
Break it and a gap arises never seen until it broke,
As the wires, when cut, are traitors to the sentence-breathing
    shock ;
Heedless of such bond of union grapple we with erring mind,
Feeling not the mighty impulse streaming from our greater kind,
Which, like to the spreading glory waiting on the dying sun,
Shoots along this link that binds us till we feel ourselves as one ;
And we grow into their triumph as their works rise up sublime,
Like a book that lies before you glowing with some poet's rhyme ;
And the spirit of the minstrel, leaping distance, shoots along,
With a monarch's footsteps ringing through the pathways of his
    song.

Thus the mighty who have labour'd in the ages sunk behind
Link their spirit to that purpose which they left among their kind ;
And forever as the groaning world tramples under foot
Hydras born of sleeping Wisdom when it pleas'd her to be mute ;
And wherever slow Improvement wanders with a laggard's pace—
Like the Cynic with his lantern roaming in the market-place—
There their power of brain is busy, bringing with its potent rod
Genii from all points of heaven, and set them working with a nod.
In the whirl and sweep of traffic, in the long and restless street,
Multitudinous with echoes ringing from a thousand feet ;
In the clash and clank of hammers, in the anvil's busy sound,
In the belt that like a serpent whirls in hot pursuit around ;
In the crash of tooth and pinion slowly forming linkèd rounds ;
In the mighty beam that labours, like a Hercules set in bounds ;
In the slightest puff of steam that specks the ocean far away ;
In the sail that boasts a shadow hanging in the lucent bay ;
In the furnace darting upward glowing gleams to greet the skies,
Till they start at such a welcome with a flush of red surprise ;
In whatever rises up for myriad use with loud acclaim ;
In whatever sets for Progress stepping-stones to reach her aim.

But it hath a deeper meaning, and a broader strength and skill,
In the clanking of the rail, and in the engine's thunder still;
For the might of what our fellows can with cunning fingers frame
Moves with him as on he flashes in great bursts of smoke and
        flame.
Lo, at times as on he strides a quick and glowing frenzy steals
From his sinews swift as light, and from the roar and rush of
        wheels,
Quick as when the far-off mountains shake themselves from summer
        mist,
Or the virtue to the woman when she touch'd the hem of Christ—
Filling all the soul within me with a wonder at my kind,
And the nerve and battle onward of this ever-restless mind.
In such fits and heats I wander half a step before the years,
Taking to myself the vision forethought sets apart for seers;
And I see a healthier colour, promise of a Titan's prime,
And a mightier sinew working on the naked arm of Time;
And behind him roars nor cannon, nor the champ of fretting steed,
But the nations leaning forward ready for the swordless deed.
But he waves them back and questions, "Am not I the thought
        and type
That shall shake the perfect blossom, knowing when the seed is
        ripe?
Am I not the unseen symbol giving every moment birth,
Breathing with a finger resting on the iron pulse of earth,
Waiting till I feel a calmer action in the glowing vein,
And a wider stretch of bosom ere I stoop to sow the grain?"
This he whispers, and forever as he shakes his restless wings
Silent sands within his hour-glass slip away like human things.
But the cycles hid behind him, peering from their shadows still,
Wear upon their brow a purpose which they tremble to fulfil;
Then, for songs to hail their coming, lyrics from some burning
        heart
Beating with the perfect mission, glowing with the given art.
Higher task is not for poets than to touch with sounding chords
Mighty Memnons of advance, and shape their whispers into words.
This the task for which the laurel glitters, as upon the thorn
Woven webs of silky slightness swaying in the flush of morn.
Let him take such wreath unblushing, knowing that it is his right,
But his inspiration only as he feels his given might.
Then, when round his brow its coolness circles with inspiring clasp,
Let his thoughts take deeper music, wider range, and higher grasp;

Let him sing the better yearning running through our noble strife,
As from bough to bough the juices creeping start the buds to life ;
And the promise growing fuller with the rounding of each year—
O, the future is a giant. 'Tis his shadow we have here !

What though Science fills her nectar lavishly in golden cups,
And the earth like a Bacchante all unwitting reels and sups ;
She is yet a village maiden, Nature touching not her life,
Girt in dreams of busy childhood, knowing not the aim of wife ;
Wearing simple vesture loose in fold that opens to disclose
Breasts that nurse a wish to blossom like the twin buds of a rose.
Then what wonders will they suckle when the juices in her blood
Slowly swell their balmy outline to the round of womanhood :
Like the gods that from Olympus stole into the arms of earth,
Made their nature as a mortal's, and a monster was the birth ;
So the thought and might of doing, slipping into her embrace,
Shall be fruitful, and a wonder help the labour of our race.
But from him of double semblance shall she keep the wish'd-for
    prize,
Heeding not the shallow purpose peering out from narrow eyes ;
But to him who toils and battles with an earnest, broad desire,
She shall give her fruitful favours, and our fellows shall be higher—
Higher in the broader feeling, in the wider aims that come,
Pledging all their good to mankind, ever potent, ever dumb.
They shall ride, like one in armour, through the wastes and fens of
    life,
Giving battle wherever error rears a lance and shield for strife.
They shall usher in the primal order of the happy earth,
Working with their cunning only that a good may be the birth.

This shall Science do as earnest of her firm and matron prime,
When her passion fruits are growing strong in limb to wrestle
    time ;
They shall watch her slightest motion as she lifts her magic wand,
Rush like Ariels at her nod, and roll the earth into her hand.
Who are they that curb their vision, lifting up with finger tips
Coloured glass and watch her crying that she reels into eclipse ?
Narrow hearts that will not widen, souls that in their shells of clay
Flicker up like feeble tapers, but to pass in smoke away ;
Prophets that should walk this world with their evil croakings
    wrung
As the shadows swept by Dante in the hell he made and sung ;

Ghostly faces looking backward through the shadows thick and
    vast,
Like Remorse upon a deathbed writhing round to view the past.
Such should be their doom who torture Wisdom into selfish deeds,
Deeming that the earth should wither to give space to sow their
    creeds.
This were faith in scope and keeping with the brute's within his
    den ;
Let them give their creeds to idiots, but the world unto men :
What is all this flash of triumph, from our very footsteps brought,
But the promise of a brighter lying yet unknown to thought—
Brighter in the strength to usher in the many varied use,
As a single bud foreruns a thousand forming in the juice.
Yet we grow apace and prosper : All that hath a strength and
    nerve
Is, like Samson taken captive, made to bow the knee and serve ;
And we peer with deepest cunning into seeming useless things,
Train them to a little method, and a miracle upsprings.
Lo, the motion of a finger trifling with a simple wire
Shakes the nations into whispers ere a moment can expire ;
And a slight and simple needle shaking in its paltry case
Turns the boundless stretch of ocean to a fearless dwelling-place.
Thus we overleap those wonders kept by ever niggard time,
Heirlooms of the early worlds in the acmè of their prime ;
Ah, if they could look upon us from the gloom and dust of years,
Feel our mighty grasp and purpose as the goal we strive for nears ;
See the very germ, yet hidden when they pass'd in death away,
Growing into perfect blossom with their fellows yet in clay—
Think you would they turn in wonder to the calm of their abodes,
Blush at all their strength, and worship those who toil'd below as gods?

This is but a wilder fancy creeping through our rugged song ;
Yet a burst of rhythmic madness cannot do our fellows wrong,
For in them is nerve and action, will to do and will to dare,
And the demons of their magic work their wonders everywhere.
Hark ! as onward rolls the world with a rough and toiling sound,
All their voices swell and mingle in triumphal hymns around.
Come they from the dash of paddles urging through the spray and
     ·   foam,
Freights of earnest bosoms outward, freights of smiling faces home ;
From the lunge of pistons working scant of room to breathe and pant,
Yet like slaves do all the feats their ever cunning masters want ;

From the whirring of the spindle in the hot and dusty room,
From the mazes of the wheel, and from the complicated loom,
From the furnace belching outward molten forms at their desire,
Like Enceladus upspringing through his hill of smoke and fire :
Mighty sounds are these, but mightier rush with everlasting hail
From the thunder of the engine and the clanking of the rail.
Ah ! the monster that shall mould and make the coming cycles
    strong—
Shame on me that could desert the inspiration of my song !
So, another pæan, Brothers, ere the fancy sinks away,
Ere we take the voiceless measure ranging through our toiling day.

Arm to arm, and lay the metals, glowing but with one desire—
To do honour to the mightiest of the worshippers of fire.
All the great in early fable, mighty-pulsing Anakim,
All the thew'd and swarthy Cyclops are as nothing unto him.
Yet he seeks our aid and mutters, shaking in his sudden wrath—
Give me but a hand to guide me, give me but a fitting path.
And he foams and shrieks in triumph as at every bound and rasp,
Like twin threads laid out in distance, all the iron meets his grasp.
Dare we, then, as unto mortals, whisper fear and death to him,
When such breadth of nerve like lightning flashes through his
    heart and limb ;
When, within his throbbing bosom, bound with glowing links of fire,
Lies his wildest being panting with the thoughts that cannot tire ;
And they hiss, and leap, and flicker, licking up with fiery breath
Strength to feed his sinews working like the flash of swords
    beneath ?
O, I rise from out my weakness as he flares along my view,
And I deem that I am mighty in the labour others do ;
For the Frankensteins who made him part by part and limb by
    limb
Had the same soul beating in them as my own at seeing him.
Arm to arm, then, lay the metals, let him roll along the rods,
Like Prometheus through the heavens rushing from the angry gods.
Lo ! I look into the ages that in spirit we may see
When the hand of death hath stripp'd us from this warp of action
    free,
And I see this monster stretching his untiring sinews still,
Keeping all his strength, but blindly giving unto men his will ;
And they—restless, feeble puppets—he not deeming them as such,
Move his iron footsteps onward with a paltry finger touch ;

And they link him unto wonders, and their triumphs still increase
Till some awe-struck fellow whispers " It were time for us to cease."
But they turn and shout an answer, high rebuke in all its tone,
"Shame, and have another planet growing mightier than our own
Out on such a craven's whisper, all unworthy of our powers,
And this monster toiling with us, making all his being ours.
Forward, then, and let us fashion wider space for his career,
Till the old earth reels and staggers as his sounding footsteps near."
Then they turn to all their labour, shaping as their thought will
    speak
Pathways into which he glides with iron grasp and madden'd
    shriek ;
And forever as their success brings a wilder aim in view,
Flashes out by fits a wonder at the miracles they do.
Said we not the future's shadow only falls upon us here
As a cloud's upon a hill when all the rest is shining clear ?
But to them, our larger fellows of the ages yet to be,
He shall rise, as gods are statured, huge of limb, and broad, and
    free ;
And in frenzy they shall hail him, bring their trophies to his feet,
Then rush on in throngs, and strive to make their wondrous gains
    complete :
While through all their fret and hurry he, the monster of our song,
With the spot of the Immortals shall in thunder flash along,
Clasping all things in his vigour, as a serpent flings his coil,
Labour's mightiest Epic rolling through the world's heart of toil.

A LOVE RETROSPECT.

"O meines Lebens goldne zeit."—*Schiller.*

THE youth of love and madness! let me sing **another song**
Ere the cynic grows upon me, and I do the world **wrong.**

Silver moonlight sleeping over fairy realms to human eyes,
Like the garments of an angel trailing from the starry skies;
Shadows lying in the distance, balmy **as** the **breath** of winds;
Moonbeams stealing sweetly through **them, like the thoughts**
    through poets' minds;
River with its thousand wavelets gliding bright as silver bars,
With a quiet stretch of bosom for the holding of the **stars.**
Not a sound to fret the silence—all **as still** as still **can** be,
Save at times a low faint murmur from the trembling aspen tree.

I, a poet, here am waiting, in the hush of all this night,
For the glimmer of a maiden, and the sound of footsteps light;
Oh she tarries, and I weary, and the hours are strangely long—
I will slip into the silence, and be busy with a song:

Come, O heart, within **this** bosom downward **from thy** purple
    throne,
Take a happy blushing maid, and set her in thy stead thereon;
Then let all thy purest being ever watch **her, as** above
Glows and gleams **the** wingèd cherub **angel of the passions—Love.**
Thou shalt guide her feet **in pathways that shall lead to** quiet
    days,
Drink **the** tearlike raptures **from her eyes, and** think **it noble**
    praise;
And thy soul shall **be a** mirror, taking **every mood** of hers,
While the thoughts that stir thy pulses—let them bow **her**
    worshippers,
· **She** shall pay thee back in blessings manifold through all thy life—
Stand upon the hearth, an angel smiling when you call her "wife."
Then the faith that works within thee shall have firmer root and soil,
And the heavens above come nearer as you both together toil.
Both thy lives shall mix and mingle as two rivers rush in one—
Deeper grows the channel, smoother all the happy waters run.

Hush, my heart ; with all this lyric, lo ! as stately as the trees
Comes the maiden, with a presence sweeter than a meadow breeze.
"Moon, that walkest like a queen through all the bowing stars above,
Veil thine eyes, nor from thy heaven look upon a mortal's love."
All the shadows round me brighten, earth grows sweet with sudden
        charms,
As the maiden, like a goddess, sinks into my circling arms.
O, the clasp, and kiss, and bosom throbbing with its new delight !
"Turn thy face, and let me, dearest, look into thine eyes to-night.
Lo ! within their depths, like richest pearl, what is it I see ?—
Something that, like music, whispers all thy woman's love for me—
Rapt-like dreams of blissful fancies—visions of a golden time
Ranging through the years in distance with the cadence of a rhyme—
Many wealths of happiest promise, glowing like celestial fire—
Golden blossoms, slowly filling out to garner in desire.
Never sweeter poet's volume, throbbing with his passionate life—
Every tender glance within them breathing of the future wife."

Then I clasp the maiden closer with her trembling hand in mine,
And her balmy breath comes upward, like an incense from a shrine ;
Then a wind that all unweary, though the others are at rest,
Comes, and, softer than the moonlight, flings her curls upon my
        breast.
Slowly creeps her arm around me—slowly as a summer's dawn
Slips along the dreamy hills, and all the night is half-withdrawn ;
Happy stars look downward, wearing all their soft and holy looks,
While the river keeps its murmur to the compass of a brook's.
Trees wake up and whisper, " Kingdoms are not worth a maiden's
        truth ;"
(This, I tell you, this was only in my unsuspicious youth).
Then I shake apart the curls that clasp and nestle on her brow,
Kiss its warmth, and whisper fondly in her ear a lover's vow—
"Turn thine eyes to mine, and, sweetest, see as on some sacred
        shrine,
All the best of my existence yearning to be knit to thine.
Have I not a love within me, rolling like a boundless sea,
Bearing all my willing being, like a pilgrim, unto thee ?
Dost thou love me, as I love thee, with a soul that in its place
Gleams like some great star in heaven looking down upon thy face,
With a soul that knows not self, but restless still will fret and
        roam,
Flinging all its chambers open"—Enter thou into thy home.

Then I clasp the maiden closer, while her breath grows thick with
    sighs,
And upon her eyelids slumbers light, as if from Paradise.
" Shall this bosom," thus I whisper, " with its rich pulsations rife,
Scatter music like a heaven through the stretches of my life ;
Shall it keep its tone through all the trying change of good and
    ill,
Pass beyond this life, and tremble with a finer rapture still ?"
Then I wait her answer, as in temples wrought with wealth and care,
Hung the Greeks to hear the thunder of the gods that took their
    prayer.
Slowly droops her eyelids downward, as through rich and glowing
    light,
Drops a bird of sombre plumage in a long and steady flight ;
Still she will not make reply, but, in the silence soft and meek,
Lays a moment's gentle pressure of her lips against my cheek.
O the bliss and warmth of lips that tremble with a maiden's truth
(This, I tell you, this was only in my unsuspicious youth).
Then I lift her forehead upward from its wavy wealth of hair,
Look again into her eyes, and kiss the love that glimmers there.
All the stars look downward, smiling, while the pulse of Nature
    seems
Beating like the fairy murmurs heard in summer noonday dreams.
Then again I question—" Dearest, with thy very heart to mine,
And thine arms enwoven round me like twin branches of a vine—
Who is he that through the pathways which thy glowing love hath
    wrought,
Ranges, culling all the fancies of thine hours of sweetest thought ?"
Droops her blushing forehead slowly downward that I may not see,
As she whisper'd in a very heaven of murmurs, " None but thee !"
O the power of love and madness ! O the pulse and strength of
    youth !
O the soul that melts like sunset in a maiden's eyes of truth !
Could I paint you then my feelings, fling the veil from off my soul,
Show you all the dreams that shook me like a sudden thunder roll ;
You would hold me but for jests, and twit me on the finer chords,
Crying, with uplifted finger—" Lo ! a fool of woman's words."
" Ay, a woman's words," I answer, " they were pearls unto me,
And my life shot from its darkness like a light from out the sea.
I had strength to scale Olympus, will to dare the task alone.
Fling the bolts about like firebrands, hurl the Thunderer from his
    throne ;

Make the very heavens tremble, like a landscape in the heat ;
Gather worlds in like worthless things, and fling them at her feet.
Even Nature shared my frenzy, and the stars in ecstasies
Leapt, as shaken in their dwellings by some all-ethereal breeze ;
Every whisper from the tree and chirp from bird but half asleep ;
Every murmur from the river gleaming in the distance deep ;
Every moonbeam coming down in smiles to wander far and wide—
Each and all had fingers pointing to the maiden by my side."

O ! ye smile at all the madness of this only love of mine,
But the past still glows above it like the fire on Abel's shrine ;
Still it studs my life, like some great temple built by Pagan hands,
Or the vacant Sphinx, forever gazing over Egypt's sands.
Unvergesslich on its forehead write I with my bitter tears,
While a sallow look discolours all the foremost of the years.
Can it be the single cloud seen from the Carmel of the mind,
Or the donning of the armour for the war with human kind ?
Let such shadows sink, for truly all the world was fair and wise,
When the strength of eighteen summers look'd into a maiden's eyes.

JOHN KEATS.

"He is made one with Nature ; there is heard
His voice in all her music."—*Shelley.*

THERE be more things within that far-off breast,
    Whereon the flowers grow
Of the boy poet, in his Roman rest,
    Than hearts like ours can know.

He slumbers, but his sleep hath not our fears,
    For all aside is thrown ;
And from the gateway of his tombèd years
    A power is moving on.

And in that power is hid a voice that speaks
    To hearts that throb and rise
From common earth, and worship that which seeks
    The wider sympathies.

For he is silent not ; and from the bounds
    Wherein his footsteps move
Come, like the winds at morn, all summer sounds
    Of boyhood thought and love.

So he to us is as an oracle
    Whose words bedrip with youth ;
The latest spirit, bathing in the well
    Of Pagan shape and truth.

A passionate existence which we scan ;
    But first must lay aside
The rougher thinking that belongs to man,
    And take the unsettled pride

Of eager youth and fancy, and a strength
    Misled by the fond zeal ;
For Grecian look and light yet found at length
    The power to touch and feel.

So, taking this into thy thought, you trace
    His wealth of opening lore ;
He bursts upon you with his freshest grace,
    And moves a man no more—

But a bright shadow in the heart's expanse,
    Crown'd with the tenderest rays
Of love, and thought as of the far-off glance
    Of early summer days.

So bring him from beneath the sky of Rome,
    From all her youngest flowers.
I weep that there his dust should find a home,
    And all his spirit ours !

But no, you cannot ; for a bond he keeps
    Whose ties are firmly strung—
The lone yet passionate heart of Shelley sleeps
    Beside the dust he sung.

And it were vain to leave him there and foil
    His rest—so let them sleep

Within the silence of that glorious soil,
    Whose inspirations steep

Their songs in colours like the summer boughs—
    Whose freshness ever strives
And blooms, like asphodels, upon the brows
    Of two immortal lives.

And there they sleep, as if their fates had said
    They shall not sleep alone ;
The singer and the sung must fill one bed,
    And make their ashes one.

It is so ; and through the quick years that roll,
    That sepulchre of theirs
Is as a passionate and wish'd-for goal
    To which all thought repairs—

While in our hearts, as is their dust at Rome,
    Their spirits feel no wrong ;
But shine to us like gods serenely from
    The Pantheon of Song.

THE MOTHER AND THE ANGEL.

First appeared in *Good Words*, and taken from that **Magazine** by kind permission of Messrs Strahan & Co.

" I WANT my child," the mother said, as through
    The deep sweet air of purple-breathing morn
She rose mid clouds of most celestial hue,
    By the soft strength of angels' wings upborne.

Then he who bore her to her heavenly rest
    Drew back the hand that hid her weeping eyes,
And said, " I cannot alter the request
    Of Him whose glory lights the earth and skies.

" For ere I came, and, as I paused again,
    To hear His omnipresent words, He said,
' Take thou the root, but let the bud remain,
    To perfect into blossom in its stead.'

" And so I bear thee, that in our sweet land
    You may be one of our immortal kind,
With not one task but to reach forth thy hand
    And guide the footsteps of thy child behind."

He ceased, and winging, reach'd those realms on high,
    Whose lustre we half see through stars below,
And all the light that fills our earthly sky
    Is but a shadow to its mighty glow.

Now whether that the mother in this light
    Stood yearning for her treasure in our hands,
Or whether God saw fitting in His might
    To reunite again the broken bands

We know not ; but when night had come at last,
    And wore to clasp the first embrace of day,
An angel enter'd, though the door was fast,
    And all unseen took what we held away.

One took the mother from all earthly claim,
    From out the bounds of life and all its harms ;
But still I think 'twas God Himself that came,
    And took the child and laid it in her arms.

THE DEAD CHILD.

" All its innocent thoughts,
Like rose leaves scattered."—*Wilson.*

THERE is an angel sleeping in this room,
  A little angel, with the quietest bloom
  Of white, all downy-like, upon the cheek
And round the brow ; and yet it will not speak,
Though the small lips retain the hues from which
We fondly wish the eloquence of speech ;

B

But in its silence seeming still a form
Cut by some sculptor when his mind was warm
With highest beauty. Look ! I pull away
The little curtain, and you look on clay,
Yet clay so wrought to love's own rest that you
But weep to share the calm that meets your view,
Then worship, and with fingers fondly touch
The little brow that wakens not at such ;
Put back the delicate wealth of silken hair,
And wonder why it keeps so fresh and fair ;
Kiss the faint curvèd lips, and you the while,
A dupe to fancy, think they sweetly smile ;
Press the shut eyelids, that, all white and even,
Like tiny clouds that hide blue spots of heaven,
Droop o'er those eyes, whose light has fled away,
To leave this human blossom to decay,
Like the few flowers that yet seem dewy fair
Within the little hands. We placed them there,
As if to see how well their hues would keep,
A perfect type of its most innocent sleep.
But these will wither, and the grave will hide
Within its dull, dank, clasp our household pride,
And little feet will touch no more the hearth,
And little lips will laugh no more their mirth,
But silence, ever deeper when we miss
A cherub presence for its nightly kiss.
Yet in our hearts' most sacred spot shall be
A little angel type of this we see—
Fair, pure, and heavenly, through the changing years,
And kept all golden with our sweetest tears,
Until the little form, not lost, but hid
Far in our bosom like a golden thread,
Shall twine itself around our life till we
Bear lighter weight of sin and earth, and see
Before us all our paths shaped out by love,
And brighten'd with a shadow from above,
Beneath whose balm and Hope's eternal tone
The days but seem as links to guide us on.
Till, when we reach our pilgrimage of clay,
And all we had of earth is pass'd away,
We find at last beyond the stars' abode
Our little wither'd bud full blown in God.

THE AUTUMN WALK.

I WALK through the golden autumn wood
 When the leaves are in their decay :
And my heart leaps into its solemn mood
 As they wither and drop away.

For I think that this life of ours is a tree,
 And the leaves are each fresh green hope,
That we keep like the dream of the good to be
 For the blossoms that yet will ope.

And I know that the years are the slow sure frost
 That will nip with a bitter breath
The sweet green buds, till their bloom be lost
 In a shadow like that of death.

Then woe unto him that, when thus bereft,
 And the drear cold gust hath pas'd,
Looks within and can see no leaflet left
 That might gladden his eyes at last.

What comfort will lie in the claspèd hands,
 In the look of doubt and woe,
While the heart in its own deep shadow stands
 Looking down at its leaves below ?

Ah, no ! like the tree that I stand beneath,
 That, though wither'd, and black, and bare,
Still keeps one leaf that hath stood the breath
 Of the cold and unkindly air :

May I thus so stand when my heart pours down
 Its leaves all sear'd and dry,
Keeping still one leaf though the rest be flown,
 And that leaf—my hope on high.

ELIORE.

YOUNG Eliore lay dreaming, and the light
Of the young sun came in, and angel bright
It made her, as within her golden hair
It stole in smiles, and gladly slumber'd there,
Making her head one beaming light and love,
As in our dreams we see the blest above.
She slept the rosy sleep of life and breath—
The other paler sleep we call it death—
But hers was of that joyous time when years
Crown the full heart with tenderness and tears,
And we perforce must dream of all those things
That wave before us bright as angels' wings—
Visions that come from higher worlds, whose tone
Lives for a moment to exalt our own.
Sweet time, when, hardly conscious of a sin,
We paint the world as we feel within,
And dream like Eliore, whose breasts' sweet swell
Rose with her breathing, with her breathing fell;
While on her lips, moist with her purity,
A smile lay soft as woman's smiles can be,
Touch'd into life with the pure thoughts that keep
Their home in virgin bosoms—Let her sleep.

Young Eliore rose up, and, glad and gay,
Look'd from the window on her bridal day—
Her bridal day, in which her maiden life
Would culminate into the novel wife, •
And bring new dreams to crown the quiet bliss
When her sweet lips would falter forth their Yes.
And she would hear *him* whisper in her ear
All tender vows, that none but she might hear,
As looking meekly up, in mute surprise,
Catch all the lover husband in his eyes.
Thus thought she; and she smiled as each new dream
Came up to cheer her with its tender beam,
Till, as she turn'd, she saw, full-blown and fair,
A rose that by the window blossom'd there,

So put her hand forth to possess its bloom ;
But ere she reach'd it, like a sudden doom
The leaves fell withering at her feet, and lay
Still as the shadows of a summer day.
Then in a moment every happy thought
Sank in the horror that the omen brought,
And her eyes droop'd, while from the downcast face
All joy had fled, and grief was in its place ;
And her crush'd heart beat fainter as she stood.   ·
Half-lifeless in her chamber's solitude.

Might she not thus be snatch'd from life's sweet pow'r,
And droop, all stricken, like this blighted flow'r,
Even on this morn, her happy bridal day,
When all her hopes seem'd perfect in the ray
Of coming bliss, and her delighted eyes
Saw all in view her earthly Paradise

Away, dread shadows ! nor with baleful breath
Pour on her heart the taint of early death,
Nor mix in such a gala hour as this
Your saddening hints with those of fairy bliss ;
For, hark ! glad voices call her, and light feet
Come tripping up, and make the echoes sweet.
They come, the bridesmaids, to array the bride,
And touch her beauty to a fresher pride.
Then let all tears be dry save those of joy,
And omens sink with all their base alloy.
Who would in such sweet moments bid their gloom
Live on, to dull the splendour and the bloom
Of the first feelings that to the pure air
Breathe forth their light as if a god were there ?
Mute touches from a heaven that glides away
When we wake up and feel that we are clay.
How beautiful was Eliore ! Her dress
Was one that set off all her loveliness.
Pure white, that, like a balmy summer mist,
Clung lovingly around her form, and kiss'd
The ground beneath.   And in her hair was set
A rose new-cull'd, whose tiny leaves were wet
With a most tear-like dewiness, that shed
A queen-like lustre on the noble head,
And on the long rich tresses that fell o'er
Her shoulders, that were whiter than the core

Of a great drift of snow, and rich and rife,
But touch'd her bosom, and grew into life
With a continuous motion, as if there
Cupid had nestling stole, and, unaware,
Betray'd with gentle thrills his resting-place;
While in the smiles that play'd upon her face
There seem'd no token of the morning dread,
But joy and happiness was there instead,
Beaming from eyes whose every glance was bright
With lustre like to Heaven's own living light.

And now the rite was o'er, and the sweet strife
Of murmur'd words whose music made her wife,
And guests had wish'd her happiness, and all
That can of good to earthly beings fall,
And *he* was at her side for whom her heart
Had beat those vows that only could depart
With death itself, if death could so untie
Those links that seem for all eternity;
And she was happy, and around the room
Her bright eyes wander'd, while a higher bloom
Grew on her cheek, as still his manly tone
Lived in her ear and mingled with her own.
Sweet moments these; but, like a flash of light,
A change came o'er her, and her cheek grew white,
And her eyes dimm'd, and tremblingly the lid
Fell slowly down, and all their lustre hid,
And she, half-sunk, ere he who sat beside
Could turn and clasp unto his breast his bride—
His bride no more; for all her love's sweet faith
Fell on his lips in one long passionate breath—
Such breath the spirit utters when it leaves
Its earthly dwelling, and in leaving grieves.
Then her arms lost their pressure, and her head
Fell forward on his bosom. She was dead.

Young Eliore lay sleeping, and the night
Came slowly in and stole away the light,
But still upon that fair young face there shone
A light the darkness had no power upon—
As if the earthly and the heavenly light
Were still to be apart, nor could unite,

For heaven, **that** we deem so far away,
Comes down to place **its** seal upon the clay,
Stamping such sweetness **on** the brow and lips
That we bless death for bringing such eclipse,
And we could weep but for the sacred hush
That floats o'er all. And so in awe we crush
All feelings into **one, and bear within**
A power to worship **with less weight of sin.**
She slept the sleep that **hath no** need of breath—
The calm, long sleep we mortals know by death,
Or silence, for such name is fit for clay
When life has shrunk in purple streams away.
A bride at morn, aflush with life's sweet thrill—
A bride even yet, **but ah ! how pale and still**
And **mute** those lips, **whose music now no more**
Might sound for human ear **on earthly shore !**
And motionless those **hands, that on her breast**
Were folded there in an eternal rest,
And stirless underneath the heart **that now**
Could trace no happy flight across the **brow,**
Or touch the cheek, upon **whose** paleness lay
The tears of human grief for human **clay,**
That, leaving the full heart all **feeling there,**
For want of such sweet **freshness were** despair.
But sacred be such grief, nor let an eye
Save that of angel view it from on high ;
But let the shadows enter in and hide
The mourning husband and the lifeless bride
Waiting for the lone grave, and still in view ·
The rose upon her forehead—wither'd too.

THE POET'S MISSION.

WOULD you hear the poet's mission ? When the gods lean from above,
    Placing in his heart the wisdom and the music that they love,
Thus they whisper, while the laurel clasps his forehead like a belt,
All their **inspiration to him, still unseen,** but ever felt :

" Go thou forth, and with thy fellows toil and cheer and sing and
    live,
For thy lips have felt the magic which to few we care to give,
And thine eyes have other vision, looking far into the years,
And thy heart a deeper insight into human life and fears ;
Oracles to shape and utter to thy toiling fellow-kind
Are upon thy lips, to lift them upward to the wider mind—
Upward to the truth and silence giving birth to fitting deeds,
And the purposes that look beyond the useless film of creeds—
Purposes that yearn to usher in the firm result of good,
Till the systems shake and settle into world-brotherhood ;
Thou shalt sing this in thy lyrics, knowing we who watch above
Care but for the proper guiding of the music that we love.
Shame to him whose lips are touch'd, yet takes his common life
    again,
Heedless of the earnest mission which through him we speak to
    men :
All the laurel on his brow shall wither, and within his heart
Gilded things shall take their place, and into hollow laughter start ;
He shall claim no meed of prophet, and his voice be as a sound
Coming from all points of heaven, and unto aimless visions bound.
But thine office shall be greater, for each whisper of thy song
Shall have power to make thy fellows battle with eternal wrong—
Battle with all strife and faction till the coming light of good
Ushers in its many triumphs, guiltless of the taint of blood.
Then the heart shall swell and widen, and from out the sordid dust
Take no more its life, but tremble with the love it keeps in trust—
Love for better faith and action—love that works and wears away
All the grosser rinds that compass what within is finer clay.
Then shall men be to each other brothers, not in word but deed,
Shaping all their paths in forethought of a weaker fellow's need ;
Striving to be wide and useful, strong in human right and bold,
Till they seem to us like shadows of ourselves in rougher mould.
Go thou forth, then, to thy mission, knowing we who watch above
Care but for the proper guiding of the music that we love.
Sing, and make thy fellows stronger ; lift them from the earth-
    desire—
Sing, nor shame the inspiration throbbing on thy lips like fire—
Throbbing with its wealth of music, bursting out in pæans strong,
Till the world rolling onward takes its motions from thy song."

BABY'S HAIR.

TAKE the letter up with anxious eyes,
  And open it with beating heart, and there,
Within the folded sheet before me lies
  A soft and silky lock of baby's hair.

I know at once that it is baby's hair,
  For, glancing down the letter, I can see
"Dear friend—my wife—a child," and here and there
  Dashes of most paternal pride and glee.

Then, light, as when we touch some sacred thing,
  I lift it up, and in my hard, rough hand
It lies like down from off some fairy's wing
  Wafted to this dull earth from Fairyland.

Half smiling still, I think how far away
  The dear one will be safe within those arms,
That will protect it from the dull, rough day
  That looms as yet afar off with its harms :

Safe in a mother's first sweet clasp, while here
  Fresh from my toil I stand, and in my eye
A moisture slowly gathering to a tear,
  As still I gaze with half a wish to sigh.

For strange it is, I think, that here to-night
  This lock should rise up from the sheet to be
A link between a baby, frail and slight,
  And a great, rugged, bearded thing like me.

Half-puzzled still, I place the lock away,
  And read the letter, teeming with its gush
Of long-hid thoughts that now burst into day,
  And into all their new-found channels rush.

" Dearer than shining gold, because less rife,"
  Thus writes my friend, " is this one lock we send,
And dearer far than aught on earth, the life
  That God hath sent us to keep to the end.

"The dear thing came as all His blessings do,
  In the lone night, as if He wish'd to teach
That when no light could greet our human view,
  The heart would know the season to beseech.

"So with this gift to open up our hearts,
  Life fills with purer aims, for this sweet link
Reaches out to the future, and imparts
  A colour unto all we speak and think.

" Truly it hath been said by one great mind *
  That God is near us when a child is born,
Giving us thoughts that grow, until we find
  Wide space for love, and none for hate and scorn.

" I feel this even now," thus ends my friend,
  " For looking on the dear, sweet face, I know
That love must move us onward to the end,
  Flowering when the frail dust is laid below."

Thanks, then, dear friend, for this, and with them take
  My earnest wishes that this life may be
Dealt out to thy sweet one, even for thy sake,
  Soft as its little silky lock with me.

THE DEIL'S IN THAT BIT BAIRN.

THE deil's in that bit bairn o' mine, for every noo and than
  He gies me siccan frichts, that whiles for fear I scarce can stan';
  What pits sic mischief in his heid 'twad puzzle me to tell,
Unless to gar me start an' rin, that he may lauch himsel'.

Just noo in comin' frae the well, I heard a clash an' rair,
An' here he's wi' his heid richt through the ban's o' his wee chair;
I didna ken richt where I stood until I had him free,
An' kissin' a' his rumpled pow as he sat on my knee.

* Richter.

But 'tweel since ever **he could** crawl, an' hirstle roun' an' roun',
He aye made for that chair o' his, nod-noddin' wi' his croon ;
An' through the ban's he'd pit his heid, then start to craw an' sing,
As if he wanted **me to ken** he'd dune some michty thing.

He had some notion **o'** his ain' I pit nae doot in that,
Some queer dim **thocht** that, though a wean, he wanted **to** be at ;
But what he mean'd by't, than or noo, 'twad tak' the seven wise
    men
Wha flourished braid langsyne in Greece, to rise and let us ken.

But aye as up **the laddie** grew, his heid was growin' **tae,**
An' aye the chair **ban's** stood the same as ony ban's should dae ;
Until at last **when he boo'd** dae his muckle-thocht-o' trick,
His heid **stuck fast, an' there** he'd lie, **tae spurl** an' greet an' **kick.**

Gude kens what fash I've had since than, an' a' to little en',
For though I free his heid for **him,** it winna mak' him men' ;
I wuss when **he** grows up an' tries his ain han' shift to mak',
He maunna pit his heid through things that winna let it back.

I ken but little o' this life, it's unco ill to learn,
Yet what I hae o't gars me think the mair o' my bit bairn ;
For mony a muckle man I see, if I but turn aboot,
Wha has his heid atween **the** ban's, an' **canna get** it oot.

CHRISTMAS.

ELCOME again, O Christmas!
    Though ye come with the winter wind,
    Yet thy voice still glows and brightens,
      And thy grasp **is** strong **and** kind.

    Ye have come again, **and we listen**
      To thy lusty shout and **cheer ;**
    O, well may we **bid** you **welcome,**
      For ye bring us the glad New Year.

Then pile up the blazing fuel,
  Let the sparks flash up and go,
Till the heat spreads out, and the bosom
  Grows warm with a kindly glow:

And well may our hearts within us
  Leap up at this happy time,
When the clasp and the friendly greeting
  Are sweet as a poet's rhyme.

For ye teach, when the year is dying,
  The nobler uses of life ;
The thirst for the kindlier usage,
  And the hate for the paltrier strife.

Then, brothers, in this glad feast time
  Let us pause on the shining hearth,
And catch, in our heart's best whisper,
  The message of Christ to earth.

Lo! far through the gap of ages
  It throbs again and again,
Crying, " Peace on the earth and gladness
  To the toiling sons of men."

Aye, peace, let it come and brighten
  The world's worn weary heart,
And bring to us one broad Christmas
  That will not like this depart.

THE BURIAL OF THE OLD YEAR.

THOU midnight wind, let not a whisper wave
   The stillness all around, until we lay
   The worn Old Year within the hapless clay,
And spread with tears the turf upon his grave.

   Then this space, where worn and sear'd, like him,
      The dead leaves lie upon the sodden earth,
      No more to flutter, in their joyous mirth,
   Or send sweet music through the twilight dim—

   Here will we lay him, while the stars look down
      In tearful, silent sorrow, like our own,
      And the bare trees give forth their desolate moan,
   Wailing with naked arms all shrunk and brown.

   But first come thou, New Year, with solemn pace,
      And bend and kiss thy father on the brow,
      Place the thin hands upon the breast, and now
   Let the white head sink to its resting-place.

   Lo, far within the night, the bells begin
      To stir and peal ; but ere the dust is hid,
      Cast thou within his grave, O heart, unbid,
   All that hath secret wish for strife and sin.

   And let it with him fade away and die,
      Leaving within a wider space to sow
      The seeds of faith, whose large results we know
   Are far beyond the limits of the sky.

   So stand thou, therefore, heart, from time to time,
      Beside the graves of the dead years, and feel
      Each sin from out its earthly foothold steal,
   Leaving the path to heaven sweet to climb.

KATE.

ON New Year's Night I met with **Kate**,
    The pretty hostess of our party;
And **we were in** our palmiest state
    For mirth and fun and frolic **hearty**;
And so with quips that use made dear,
    And bouts at sharp good-humour'd banter,
We usher'd in the young New Year
    With **shouts** that **made our pulses canter.**

What riddles, too, we had to brace
    Our wits up to the point of guessing,
With now and then for breathing space
    Sweet intervals **of romp and** kissing.
Ah me ! what eyes whose tender beams
    Shot from their lashes long and shady,
So sweet, so deep, I took to dreams,
    And felt **my** heart **grow** all unsteady.

I took Kate 'neath the mistletoe,
    To give—what cannot grow too common—
A kiss; she made a feint or two,
    Then yielded like a—like **a** woman.
I bent my bearded face to touch
    Her own, upturn'd so frank and sweetly,
And, beaming with a smile, 'twas such
    That made my friendship close completely.

And then she talk'd so soft and light,
    With a voice that rang so musically,
I listen'd **as a** poet might
    To some hid stream within a valley.
I did not wish to break the spell
    That bound my head and heart together,
But wish'd within its power to dwell,
    As in the happy summer weather.

Nor could my heart refuse its share,
  But sang this snatch of song to show it.
O Kate, but thou art pure and fair,
  And, better still, you do not know it.
So sang my heart far down, the while
  She talk'd so artlessly and simple,
With still the other little smile,
  And still the other little dimple.

Ah me, but miles are now between
  Myself and Kate, to whom, dear reader,
You owe this song, that had not been
  But for each open, artless pleader,
That spoke from lip and eye ; and so
  If I, a single man, should falter—
Sub rosa—one like Kate, I know,
  Would coax me to the solemn altar.

SCHILLER AND SUNSHINE.

I LAY in the quiet sunshine
  Of the summer's golden heat ;
In my heart was the music of Schiller,
- And the dreams that this youth makes sweet :

Dreams that from their high dwelling
  Come down in the early years,
To live in our first fond worship
  Which we give with our sweetest tears.

Lo ! at every throb of the sunshine,
  As if by some magic wand,
Rose up in their beauty within me
  The dreams of the fable land ;

And each dream had a voice, and whisper'd
  With tender, confiding breath,
All the early feeling and worship
  And the joy of a simple faith.

Then my heart took a passionate longing
  To re-live that happy time,
When around my life the ideal
  Was thrown with melodious chime :

When I worshipp'd in lonely gladness
  The forms that came down to me,
And flitted before my fancy,
  And **babbled** from stream **and tree.**

Ah ! short was that boyhood worship ;
  For the voice of the toiling day
Woke me up to the labour of manhood,
  And frighten'd my dreams away.

But still in the poet's music
  Lives the flush of that happy **time,**
And still from my heart at moments
  Peals an answer to its chime.

For I lived that life in silence,
  As if speech had been a wrong,
But feeling within me the beauty
  That Schiller **has put in song.**

And strangely the poet stirr'd me
  With the magic of his line,
For I felt that his early lifetime
  Had been something akin **to** mine.

And I knew that those visions and fancies
  Were but part of the ecstacy
Lying hid in the past, and waking
  At the poet's melody.

THE SUMMER DAY.

" I speak of one, from many singled out—
One of those heavenly days that cannot die."—Wordsworth.

THERE is a lustre in the sun, a light within the sky,
I have not seen these long, long months that went so slowly by;
But I know full well what light it is, and why all things are
gay,
For this is the golden summer, and the long sweet summer day.

will not work, but fling aside all thought of daily earth,
And step into the better mind as children into birth,
And shape my life to the sweet rule that all mute things obey
In the golden days of summer, in the long, sweet summer day.

I will into the meadows green, to watch each cherish'd flow'r
Springing up like love in woman when she owns its passion'd
pow'r,
By the soft-lip'd streams that ever laugh in radiant jollity ;
Oh, the meadow flow'rs, the summer flow'rs, are glorious things to
me !

I have stood and watch'd for hours their bloom when younger
years were mine,
Yet a something lay within their tints I could not all define ;
But I view them now with riper faith, for I know that God above
Looks down with His large eyes on each, and their brightness is
His love.

I have waited for their coming when the snow lay deep and long,
As the heart will keep up yearning for some cherish'd poet's song ;
And now I leap with joy to think that all are here again,
As if angels flung them down as gifts to cheer the hearts of men.

What spirit in their pulses, and what gentle thoughts are theirs,
They will not tell to none but those that bow their worshippers ;
And so sweet their magic silence, as they peep from out their
bow'rs,
That I think the brightest spots above are set apart for flow'rs.

C

There is beauty in the long-ribb'd hills, in the valley soft and green,
In the trees that stand like sages with their shadow all between;
But a better beauty shadows all those quiet things that lie
And blush in meekness at our feet, as if loth to meet the eye.

In the balmy glow of landscape is a power that can move
All the passions to one duty, and that duty is but love;
We grow old, but this within us is a light that will not sink;
Death can only make us leap above and lift again the link.

I never saw the city but its restless tread and pain
Made me yearn to quit the tumult for the quiet fields again;
And I mutter'd, as the passion and the throb grew worse and
    worse—
"Man has set his fleeting dwelling here, and God His quiet
    curse!"

So I will unto the meadows green, and hear each mute thing
    preach,
Filling all my bosom with the lore a blade of grass can teach,
Lying by the streams until I steal a portion of their art,
And imprison all their laughter in a corner of my heart.

Work! what niggard bosom slipt to-day that thought from out its
    clasp,
As if one hour we could not fling the muck-rake from our grasp—
Why, all the earth is full of charms like a maid on her bridal day;
And shame to him that will not join one hour her roundelay.

I care not for the riches in the coffers of the great,
Nor the line that comes through the mighty years to swell a high
    estate;
Give me the faith of a poet's eye, and the thoughts that spurn
    decay,
And the light that lies in the glorious smile of the long sweet
    summer day!

THE THRUSH.

IKE the songs I have heard in childhood
   Comes thy voice, O thrush, to me,
And again in my heart leaps the promise
   Of the sunshine that shall be :

Sunshine, and joy, and splendour
   To make this earth rejoice—
O the glory of being a poet
   When such can come at thy voice ;

For with every gush of thy music
   A thrill comes down from above,
Breathing out in its softest whisper—
   Come forth to your task, O love !

Come forth, and wake up from their slumber,
   In the calm of their quiet nook,
The still dead flowers—till the primrose
   Sees its own sweet self in the brook ;

Till the violet's happy presence
   Peeps forth with an azure smile ;
And the trees burst forth in their gladness
   To a thousand buds the while ;

Till the earth smiles up to the heaven,
   And the heaven smiles down to the earth—
O the glory of being a poet,
   When thy songs call such into birth.

So I think this hour when I labour,
   If the mission came down to me,
And my lips had the touch and the music,
   I would like to sing like thee :

Sing in the gloom of my lifetime,
   As ye sing in the youth of the year,

Till the golden future grew brighter
  From the shadows around me here—

Till the hearts of my toiling fellows,
  Hearing such songs from me,
Would flush up into ampler blossom,
  As at thine wake the flower and the tree.

THE SPIRIT OF LOVE.

THE Spirit of Love came down upon the earth,
  He came full-breath'd and strong,
And ever as he went a glorious birth
  Grew forth in flowers and song.

The trees burst into buds, and in all love
  Shook forth their morning hymn,
While the white clouds kept silent watch above,
  Like veilèd cherubim.

The populous birds from out their leafy bound
  Made music everywhere,
And shook with thrills of modulated sound
  The rich and balmy air.

The brooklet, silent for a weary time,
  Broke into gush and flow,
And sang, as poets sing their first sweet rhyme,
  Its pæan soft and low.

The flowers came forth and spread, in meek surprise,
  Their hues of varied tone,
And gave, full-hearted, to the happy skies
  An incense all their own.

A murmur like a fairy's song went through
  The earth's life-heaving breast;
Then sank away, as all such murmurs do,
  In ecstacies of rest.

So where that Spirit stood, in holy mirth—
  By wood, or hill, or stream—
A smile, **as if the** sky **had** fallen **to earth,**
  Woke up with angel **beam.**

And in that smile the leaves and flowers took part,
  To make earth sweet and fair.
O Spirit of Love! come thou into **my heart**
  And make all blossom there.

OOR JOHNNIE.

WHAT lauchs o'love we **hae** at nicht wi' Johnnie, **our wee wean,**
  As he wamples aff his mither's knee **to** row **on the hearth-**
     stane ;
An' there he spurles wi' wee fat legs, an' mum'les in his **glee,**
Sweet gems frae his ain authors—Greek an' Hebrew unto **me.**

Then at anither thocht he crawls to grup me by the tae,
But when he tries to pu' me doon the bauchle comes away ;
An' owre he rows upon his back, while in his sweet blue een
The shadow o' **a tear** comes up, half frichten'd **to be seen.**

Then, if I tak' him on my knee, he's **no a moment** there
Until he pooks my beard, an' rows **his fingers in** my hair ;
Pu's at the paper that I read, **his wee lips shaped** to spell,
Then rives a column off, an' starts **an' goo-goos on himsel'.**

I whiles **think, as I watch** his pranks through a' **the** hale forenicht,
That he'll turn out some great **man yet, to** fill **us** wi' delicht ;
For big things only tak' his e'e, **and soothes** his every whim ;
What pleases ither weans at ance, gets **thraws** an' glooms frae him.

He cares na for the string o' pirns we **hing** aboot his neck ;
The ase-hole gets his rattle, an' his yellow Jumpin'-Jeck ;
He knocks his horse's head in twa, and pu's away the tail,
Then flings the rest, to hear a splash, richt in the water pail.

But lay the tangs across his legs, or sic unhandy tool,
Or let him grup the poker, or the kettle by the bool,
Then hoo he gurrs an' kicks until he raises sic a drouth,
That for ae hoor he fechts to get the fender in his mouth.

A stick's a michty prize to him, if twice as lang's himsel' ;
A wood sword gars him brichten up, an' try to cut an' fell ;
Gude keep him frae the fife an' drum, when he grows braid an'
      stark—
I wadna like tae see him list tae dae sic bluidy wark.

But far afore thae things, an' what can please him best ava,
Is breakin' ae auld bottle wi' anither perfect sma'.
This wark's an unco treat to him, an' mak's him hotch wi' glee,
An' aye at every smash he mak's he lauchs an' looks at me.

I think frae this that he'll turn oot some great teetotal han',
An' wear a gowd-bespangled bib, and head the Templar van—
Break a' the bottles labell'd *Bass*, the gill stoups bash and clour ;
Pu' doon an' split the signs, an' mak the big-wamed landlords sour.

But while I'm biggin' up my dreams the "san' man" comes at last,
An' gars him glow'r an' rub his een, then steek them firm an' fast ;
He tottles ow'r sae deep an' soun' that mak' what noise ye can
It canna steer or wauken up oor sairly tired wee man.

The poker tum'les frae his han' an' fa's upon my taes,
His wee head wabbles up an' doon as he gets aff his claes—
There, noo, a mither's kiss has seal'd the saft sleep on his e'e,
But mornin' licht 'ill bring again wee Johnnie back to me.

POETIC ASPIRATIONS.

AH me! for all my toil and search,
    And rhyming, till the muse grow surly,
  I doubt I ne'er shall hook my perch,
      But miss him like that wayward Burley,

Who fish'd and fish'd, and still would ply
  Each bait his ready fancy hit on,
And hook'd at last a paltry eye—
  But for the rest, turn up your Lytton.

It costs but little, I avow,
  To push yourself amongst your betters,
To splash with ink your massive brow,
  And dub yourself a man of letters;
But still to live and feel the scorn
  Of Fame, who never stirs a pinion,
Nor lifts with glancing eye her horn,
  To blow you through her sweet dominion.

What though you wander all alone
  And spin out poems short and pretty,
And take for mottoes to each one
  Some transcendental line from Goethe
Or Schiller, just to show you care
  A little for the higher learning,
And fling out jewels here and there
  For minds both witty and discerning?

What though your knowledge, free and far,
  Extends to bounds you may determine,
Say, from that horrid Punic war
  To that between the French and German;
And still you chuckle, and suppose
  Your fame grows wider and sublimer,
While your next neighbour, laughing, knows
  That you are but a village rhymer?

And then, with anxious heed, you get
  Your portrait in a nice position,
With head a little forward set,
  As if in some ecstatic vision;
Or leaning on your hand, with eyes
  That do their utmost to preserve a
Soft dreamy look of sweet surprise,
  As if they look'd upon Minerva.

Well, 'tis an awful thing to think
    That, after all one's firm devotion,
Not counting the expense of ink,
    Should come no grade of sweet promotion ;
And, worst of all, to know that none
    Will come to ope the muse's portals,
Though you should live a cycle done,
    Or live undying, like Swift's immortals.

I praise your Tennyson at times,
    Though, *entre nous*, within I'm frowning,
And grudge him, lucky dog, his rhymes,
    Along with those of mystic Browning ;
I only wish this envy might
    Prevail upon them to their giving
A leaf from off their laurel bright,
    To keep my poor afflatus living.

But stop ! the arts, as I have heard,
    Go round this earth in sweet gyrations,
And are by some strange luck conferr'd
    On even the most unpolish'd nations.
Then, what if they should come to me,
    Instead of barbarous climes, to show it ?
Why, I would humbly bow my knee,
    And beg them to make me a poet.

A RETROSPECTIVE ODE.

I SEE yet, bright as summer beams,
    The spot where all my childhood wander'd,
And where, in rich Arabian dreams,
    I thoughtlessly the moments squander'd ;
I see it still, the very same
    As when, a smooth-faced sturdy " duffer,"
I went to school, and, to my shame,
    Grew tired of knowledge, and had to suffer.

Ay me ! the same old happy home,
  With all its fields, and woods, and meadows,
Within whose scope for hours I'd roam,
  Or lie within their cooling shadows,
Watching with eager, anxious view
  The butterflies ; then, full of rapture,
Pick out some one of dazzling hue,
  Rush out, and make a sudden capture.

I see the lilac oak, whose wood
  Supplied me bows for all my arrows,
While I, another Robin Hood,
  Would steal a march upon the sparrows.
What havoc made I then—but now,
  When given to less hasty thinking,
I own I drew another bow,
  And told some fables without shrinking.

I fancy I can hear the brook,
  Along whose banks, with sudden yearning
To turn a Walton, I would hook
  Myself a dozen times in learning ;
But never came no trout to sight
  To gratify my zeal, that I know,
Except, at times, when I would light
  Upon some isolated minnow.

But where's the pond where, later still,
  And more expert in my researches,
I waded knee-deep with a will
  To haul out unsuspecting perches ?
Dried up, oh heart ! how things will dry
  In this cold world of ours, and vanish,
Leaving us still to mope and sigh
  O'er thoughts we fain would try to banish.

Per Bacco what a Paradise
  We leave behind us when we saunter
From happy boyhood's heavenly ties
  To manhood with a wilder canter.
But fled is all that glorious time,
  That Iris-like bound earth and heaven

Together, making all sublime
    In light from purest sources given.

But I'm forgetting all this while
    My readers—that's **if I** have any—
Would rather **wish to j**oke and smile,
    Than sigh with me a rhyming **zany.**
I **bow in deference to** this taste
    A short stiff **bow**—a little **awkward**—
And turn to finish **out in haste**
    This rhyme, begot **by looking** backward.

There, too, the long straigh**t avenue**
    In **which, with** deepest meditation,
I wander'd with this thought in view
    To startle with my rhyme a nation.
For there the muse first came, and **spread**
    Her incense, which **around** still **lingers,**
And there I shook **my** solemn head
    And counted rhymes upon **my** fingers.

What nonsense took its flight from prose
    In that sweet time when I paraded
Along its length with laurel rows
    On either side to keep me shaded
From vulgar minds that could not know
    What heavenly footsteps wander'd **near me.**
Plenty of laurel then, but **now,**
    Ah me, not even a leaf to cheer me.

But sweeter far than new-found rhyme
    Were those sweet dreams in which I panted
To make my name go down with time,
    By doing deeds the world wanted.
I thought that nothing would suffice,
    But walk o'er worlds on some high mission,
As o'er those spirits **bound in** ice
    Strode Dante **in** his awful vision.

I thought—but **if** I told you all
    The fits of that sweet time, 'twould cost a

Long rhyme, or rhymes, with those that sprawl
  Through cantos in your Ariosto.
I drop the sable veil, and sigh
  To think those dreams, now long discarded,
Should turn their backs and wish to fly
  For what? to leave us rough and bearded.

Farewell, then, oh, my boyhood's home ;
  In thee the years fled bright and splendid ;
But now to me they never come
  With such wild flush of hope attended.
And farewell, too, those dreams that pass'd
  Before me, ever fresh and novel,
Then sank away, to leave at last—
  Diavolo ! the pick and shovel.

STERNE.

I HATE your Sterne, though still at times,
  When for a lighter half-hour yearning,
I toss aside unfinish'd rhymes
  For Uncle Toby's warlike learning ;
Or sit within the bowling green,
  And slip into his soldier's fancies.
And be field-marshal of the scene,
  And note down how the siege advances.

I watch him as with quiet smile
  He looks on honest Trim parading,
Who scowls defiance all the while
  He sets himself for cannonading ;
Then, when the mimic storms begin,
  And all such military raptures,
Along with Toby I rush in,
  And fight, and make a thousand captures.

All this stirs up my bosom's fire,
  But when I count myself the winner,

Behind, with fingers on the wire,
  I see that sentimental sinner,
Cold, stiff, and harsh, and sneering **still,**
  At all my little touch of feeling,
And chuckling o'er **his studied** skill,
  That hides his flimsy double-dealing.

Then all at once, in utter wrath,
  I leap up from my seat, and **striding,**
Dismount the cannons in my path,
  Nor heed my Uncle Toby's chiding,
Nor look on Trim, who at such hap
  Turns slowly round **in** formal fashion,
Then doffs in doubt **his** favourite cap,
  And wonders at my sudden passion.

Then dries the tear about to **come**
  To grace the ass's piteous story,
And all my fine resolves **grow** dumb
  Though looking at the **captive** hoary.
I hear the starling's **"Can't get out,"**
  Nor feel one single muscle quiver,
But curse **his** noise, **and turn** about,
  And **walk away as cool as** ever.

I seldom now affect such hue,
  Even in my moments most poetic;
And still I think a time or two
  Before I make myself pathetic.
This comes of Sterne.   And **he who may**
  Still yearn **for all** his gilded bubble,
May fling his heart and purse away,
  And make that hollow "Journey" double.

OH, GLORIOUS TIME!

OH, glorious time! (my spirit thus must speak).
  The incensed breeze from every nook is blown,
And soft, as if a maiden laid her cheek
  All blushing in its warmth, against your own.

The very clouds above beseem to me
    Like spirits wander'd from a higher day,
Who, seeing all the joy that now I see,
    Drop down a tear or two, then glide away.

I hear the lark, in airy distance, pour
    His melody, full-throated, clear, and strong,
As if he knew the angels flung the door
    Of heaven open to let in his song.

And, nearer at my hand, the streamlet sings
    Its little oracles, from which the woods
Know when to don their ample blossomings,
    And flush the stillness of their solitudes.

While, like a maiden, who with stolen glance,
    Looks fondly on her lover passing by,
So peeps the violet from a quiet trance
    Of dreams, the colour of its kindred sky.

And other flowers, in unobtrusive light,
    Issue in many hues into their birth,
Seeming like God's sweet wishes, in the night,
    Flung down to all His creatures upon earth.

A gentle murmur creeps through all the bound,
    Soft as an angel's footstep, while I stand
Entranced, and listen as at some stray sound
    Of music stealing from the better land.

For each thing has a voice in this sweet day,
    And Nature, ever watchful, sets the whole
To most delicious sounds that steal away
    This mould of clay from the delighted soul.

And so my heart leaps up with joy to keep
    Its softest pulses in sweet unison,
For Nature, silent not, throughout her sleep
    Breathes forth the sweetest utterance of her own.

She hath this power which, whether from on high,
    Or from her own full bosom, breathes to those

Who watch her wonders with a quiet eye
Feelings of ample thought and sweet repose.

So she has touch'd, with all her inmost truth,
Each seeming lifeless, though not breathless thing ;
And they round into fresh and radiant youth,
Beaming like Eden in its first sweet spring.

Then come, whoever hath a love for her,
And rest within her arms this glorious day,
And be like me a silent worshipper,
Mighty in feeling, but with nought to say.

RECOLLECTIONS OF BYRON.

"Close thy Byron ; open thy Goethe."—*Carlyle.*

SOME half-a-dozen years or so,
When life had yet no crown of iron,
I took my pilgrim staff to go
And worship at the shrine of Byron ;
And there, before the mighty dead,
In hero-worship prostrate lying,
The thought first came into my head
To tell the world that I was dying.

And so, in verses neat and trim,
But with a rhythm most despairing,
I told to men and cherubim.
The sorrows of my own preparing.
I hinted how my life was gloom,
That all my hopes but came to leave me,
And wormy goals—I meant a tomb—
Could only from such ills relieve me.

I took farewell of all my friends,
In rhymes that ran to twenty verses ;
My foes, to suit their evil ends,
I left them misanthropic curses.

Then ready to give **life the slip**
    I stood ; but **ere my pulse grew** fainter,
Sat with the **sneer upon my lip**
    To some imaginary painter.

How long this might have posed **my** head
    I know not, but I thought 'twas pretty,
Till "Sartor" shook his head, **and** said,
    "**Go, shut thy** Byron, and open Goethe."
I ponder'd for a while on this,
    Then, trusting to such sage adviser,
Took Goethe, read that "Faust" **of his—**
    And, *himmel,* **am I any** wiser ?

I own my sneers have **passed** away—
    I own I never write a stanza
Beginning with " When I am clay,"
    And all your **pale** extravaganza.
But in the place of this I see
    A host of dim, chaotic fancies,
That in their **reeling seem to be**
    For ever at **Walpurgis dances.**

What good can come if I am taught
    This life is but a painted bubble ;
That after threescore years 'tis caught,
    And bursts—with nothing for your trouble ?
My curse upon **such** books **that set**
    This life in hues **to** make **one falter !**
And so I'll shift **my** worship **yet,**
    And bow before a purer altar.

LIFE AND DEATH.

I **STOOD in a** dream **between** Life and Death,
    And I whisper'd to the twain—
" **Now,** which **of** you has the sweetest faith,
    And the highest **and** surest gain ?"

Then Life, who stood at my left hand,
   Spoke out, and said to me—
" Oh, mine is the firm, free step of youth,
   And the voice of mirth and glee ;

" And mine is the friendship of heart to heart,
   And the music of happy speech ;
And mine are the customs that walk with men,
   And the social habits they teach.

" Mine, too, are the blossoms of sweet young hopes,
   And the Iris light they shed ;
And mine is the flush of the coming years,
   For I think not of the dead.

" I give the bride, in her dower of smiles,
   To the breast of him she loves,
And her sweetest thoughts owe their birth to me,
   While her heart beats like a dove's.

" I touch with a brighter look the hearth,
   And the faces that gather there,
And I lay one hand on golden locks,
   And the other on hoary hair.

" I bear in my cup, as I stride along,
   Nepenthes for care and woe;
But alas for him that will drink and keep
   His eyes still bent below."

Then Death spoke low and sweet to me,
   As he stood at my right hand—
" Oh, mine is the stirless calm of love,
   And the light of the better land ;

" And mine are the forms that have left this earth,
   The forms that you still must love.
I touch'd with my lightest touch their eyes,
   But to open them up above—

" Open them up to the light and joy,
   The blush and the golden glow—

And their beauty now is beyond that bloom
  You have set in the long ago.

" So if, in the years that have pass'd away,
  I have broken some cherish'd band,
And still in your heart you can hear a voice,
  And feel in your own a hand,

" Then come, for mine are their spirits still,
  With no touch of their earthly pain;
I sunder, and sunder but to join
  Where I cannot part again."

Then methought, as I turn'd to welcome death
  As the soother of all my fears,
I woke, and found life at my left hand,
  And my cheek was wet with tears.

JANET.

O N what part of this rough and toiling planet
  Are you now this lonely hour—sweet Janet, say?
O, tell me if you can?—alas, I cannot—
  Many long, long years have come and flown away
Since we parted from that dear old school together—
  I to sadly toil and dream in idle rhyme,
Both now weary tasks; but you, oh! tell me whither
  Tend your footsteps in this happy summer time?

Still, at moments when I slip into my trances,
  And I see the schoolhouse by the noisy stream,
Then again come back to me the happy fancies
  That of old I thought it heaven itself to dream;
Then I see you with your laughing eyes so merry,
  Blue as summer skies when all their clouds have flown;
Pouting lips that were as full as any cherry;
  Long dark hair that fell in curls so richly down.

D

Ah ! in those same blue eyes of thine how often
  Did I look and see myself within their hue,
Till I felt my own all boyish bosom soften
  With a strange, sweet, yearning tenderness for you.
Then your lightest whisper, as you sat beside me,
  Had the power to wake me with its fairy sound,
And, as soft as pinions of the angels, guide me
  To the far-off dreams within the future bound.

And, Janet, do you mind the time when sitting
  At our tasks, we then thought of no easy kind,
That you placed your arm around me, all unwitting
  Of the fingers pointed at you from behind ;
Till you heard the whisper growing loud, and, turning,
  You lisp'd out in the dear familiar tone,
" Hoots, what's aboot a cuddle ?" then with burning
  Cheek and brow half-hidden by your book, read on.

Heart ! but as I write this rhyme, again around me
  Creeps, as soft as in that day, your slender arm ;
And the magic spell that in your presence bound me
  Comes again, and all my heart grows light and warm.
I can hear no whisper, see no idle finger
  Pointed at me as I sit and dream and think,
But the silence and the bliss that still will linger
  When the past is busy with us, and we drink.

But a truce to all this fond yet foolish dreaming—
  Who knows but, as I write, that you are now
Grown into wife, and with a face all beaming
  Look upward to a broad and manly brow ;
Or sit in the long evening lightly humming
  Some early love-song that still sang of this ;
Then start to hear a well-known footstep coming,
  And hold your baby upward for a kiss ?

It were vain to wish you happy in such duty,
  If such duty now has claim'd thy gentle life ;
Yet to look again upon your ripen'd beauty—
  See how you look when blossom'd into wife ;
Sit beside you, hear your talk and merry laughter,
  Lighting up your eyes so large, and bright, and blue :

All this lives but to die a moment after,
  As the distance rises up between us two.

It may happen, then, that with such distance lying
  Between thy goings **out and** those of mine,
That I may not see you, but go onward sighing
  For the dreams a fading light has made divine ;
Yet the magic spell that in your presence **bound me**
  Shall **atone** for all when I recall to mind
How you put your little loving arm **around me**,
  In that dear old school now left so **far behind**.

THE PAIDLIN' WEAN.

OME in the hoose this moment, paidlin' oot there in the **rain**,
An', losh me ! but ae buitie on, ye limmer **o'** a wean ;
Come in an' tell me, if ye can, what great delicht ye tak'
In paidlin' in the siver till your face is perfect black ?

I canna **turn** my back, atweel, to airn your faither's sark,
But if the door be left agee, ye slip oot to your wark,
An' stamp in a' the puddles, lauchin' as they jaup an' jow,
While a' the time the careless rain pelts doon upon your pow.

See what an awfu' mess ye've made o' a' your bonnie claes,
The peenie, tae, that I pat on this mornin' when ye raise ;
'Twas white then as the new-fa'en sna', **but** noo as black's the lum,
An' what **wi'** treacly pieces, stickin' here an' there like gum.

An' noo ye maun be wash'd, nae doot, but hoo will I begin ?
I think I'll get the muckle tub, an' dook ye tae the chin ;
Dook ye ow'r the heid, ye **rogue, an'** skelp **your** hurdies tae,
An' see if that 'll mak ye ony better for the **day**.

Noo, dinna shake your curly heid, an' shape your mooth for no,
An' row yoursel' within my goon, an' lisp oot " keeky bo ;"
For sic a steerin' plague ye've turn'd, an' grown sae fierce an' croose,
That I maun try some ither plan to keep ye in the hoose.

D 2

But, losh me! even as I speak, my anger's quaten'd doon,
An' so I kiss the rosy mou' that peeps oot frae my goon;
Straik an' clap the curly heid, an' a' to fairly prove
That the anger o' a mither 's just anither name for love.

SPRING.

SPRING, come with all thy sweetest looks,
  With dewy violets in thy hair;
  Breathe balmy incense everywhere,
And strike a voice into the brooks.

Start up the life within the leaf
  And in the sloping fields, that watch
  All day the clouds, that we may catch
The coming promise of the sheaf.

Place in the woodland shadows sweet
  The simple flowers, that wile away
  The children from their happy play
And the long bustle of the street.

Fling golden bars across the sky,
  And veil the brightness of the sun,
  That we may have when day is done
The shadows that delight the eye.

Then come with gentler step and mien
  To the calm dwellings of the dead,
  There bow in love and trust thy head,
And flush their graves to brighter green.

O, SOFTLY FALLS THE MOONLIGHT.

O ! SOFTLY falls the moonlight
  On stream, and field, and tree,
But I heed not its beams that around me
  Fall as soft as soft can be :

For I know that a maiden awaits me,
  With a presence fair and bright,
And the smiles that will greet me are sweeter
  Than those of the moon to-night.

What joy will be hers when she hears me,
  What thoughts in her dark sweet eyes !
That will peep from their own sweet dwelling,
  As the stars peep down from the skies.

What idylls of happiest promise
  In their lustrous depths will gleam,
As the shadows of stars lie trembling
  In the bosom of some still stream.

O, I weary to hear the music
  Of her voice's gentle tone,
That will soften to gentle whispers
  All the roughness of my own—

That will still in my heart the yearning
  That runs through the restless day,
Till a new life starts within me,
  In place of the old away.

Then slip, O moon, from the heaven,
  Leave thy space to the stars above ;
I heed not your beams that are round me,
  I heed but my human love.

O, SUMMER DAY.

O, SUMMER day, pour down your love,
    That I may idly lie
And watch the happy clouds that move—
    The Mercuries of the sky;

Who, sent by God on some sweet task,
    Will loiter on their way,
As if they gently paused to ask
    His sanction to their stay.

I hear the birds—I see the flowers
    From their cool places peep,
And odorous as the purple hours
    That hush the sun asleep.

I hear each breathing of the wind,
    Each whisper of the tree,
That, taller than its branchy kind,
    Bows down and speaks to me.

A languor creeps throughout my blood,
    Whose happy workings move
The heart to its sublimest mood
    Of all-embracing love.

I feel no idle purpose roll
    Its restless freak in me;
But one vast wish to shoot my soul
    Through everything I see,

And be a part of this sweet light
    That warms the breathing day;
To sink from aught of mortal sight,
    And dream myself from clay.

A MEMORY.

First appeared in *Cassell's Magazine*, and taken from that Magazine by **kind permission of** Messrs Cassell, Petter, & Galpin.

S soft as an autumn leaf will light
  When the winds are hush'd and still,
Fell your hand into mine that summer night,
  When the moon rose above the hill.

And silent and pale through the holy skies
  Rose she on her starry throne ;
But I turn'd from her beams to your own sweet eyes,
  That were looking up to my own—

Looking up to my own, dear love,
  With their sweetest and tenderest glow,
As the angels may look from their home above
  On their kindred types below.

And I saw in their depths, like some glorious balm,
  All the wealth of their loving lore ;
And the thoughts in my breast grew into calm,
  That were restless an hour before ;

And the earth had a brighter look for me,
  For I saw with other eyes,
And a whisper rose up like some symphony
  Spirit-sung in paradise.

And beneath that whisper we stood nor stirr'd,
  The silence was so divine ;
While our hearts, not our lips, spoke their own sweet word,
  And your eyes look'd up to mine.

O night ! that now like a star is seen
  In the past's ever golden sky,
Come back with the joy and the thrill that have been,
  And that dear love-melody.

And it comes again with its magic tone,
  And the stars come out to teach,
And your hand falls as light as a leaf in my own,
  And our eyes look into each.

Then the thoughts that are restless in my breast
  Grow as still as still may be ;
And my heart feels the calm of thine own sweet rest,
  And that dear love-melody.

So whenever my life will droop and pine,
  And my thoughts rush to and fro,
Then I dream that your hand slips into mine
  As it did in the long ago.

AGNES.

A Study from Dickens.

IN quiet moments, when my thoughts depart
  For their sweet home within the silent land,
A maiden rises far within my heart,
  And points in silence with uplifted hand :

Points with uplifted hand to the blue skies
  That beam in sunny glory far above,
And on her brow their light, and in her eyes
  The glow of ever deep and patient love.

Then soft, as if beneath some holy balm,
  I whisper, "Agnes, O my soul," and she
Turns for a moment in her saint-like calm,
  And smiles her old sweet smile, and looks at me.

Ah, in that look how much of womanly power
  And truth and trust is hid, to fall, like rain
When summer fields await such quick'ning dower,
  On some worn human breast, to still its pain.

And all my being feeling this, I bow
   Before the maiden as she stands, and take
My life's sure guidance from her noble brow,
   That wears its soft compassion for my sake.

So Agnes claims my love, for still she seems
   Girt in her youth and truth and purer day;
The sweetest of the mighty Master's dreams
   He gave to time before he pass'd away.

Therefore, O Agnes! stand thou in my heart,
   Breathing around thee all thy trust and love,
And pointing upward when life's hopes depart
   To other realms in endless life above.

O, GLAD NEW YEAR.

GLAD New Year, with what a wealth of hope
   Thou comest to the world of toiling men,
Bringing glad days that proffer strength and scope
   For earnest thought and noble work again.

Thou wearest on thy young, smooth brow a smile
   Of happy peace and joy and tender love,
Speaking in soft yet earnest tones the while
   The eternal message utter'd from above:

Holiest of messages that come from high,
   Teaching that earth is but the vantage ground
For men to reach the fadeless things that lie
   With God, beyond this dim and earthly bound:

Sending in deep, full whispers through the breast
   The impulses for higher range and trust,
That hold this earth is not for sloth and rest,
   But for all labour till we turn to dust:

Speaking of toil, too, none may idly shun,
   But each work at his part, and bear within

All kindlier feeling for the weaker one
  Who in life's tide still struggles on to win.

O, if such message in the human heart
  Could find fit resting-place, until it knew
Its tasks, how would the better nature start,
  And tint the earth again with primal hue !

Yet come thou to us, happy young New Year,
  Fresh in thy new birth from the womb of Time ;
And work, O heart of mine, till fair and clear
  Thy tasks grow up, and with them higher climb.

FRANKENSTEIN.

IN my boyhood time long years ago,
    When life was half divine,
  I read, with a horror you may not know,
    The story of Frankenstein—

That student wild and deep who wrought
    Alone in his silent room,
Till the monster-man of his midnight thought
    Took shape in the ghostly gloom.

Then when life woke up in each heavy limb,
    And the pulses began to play,
And its dull, blank eyes open'd up on him,
    He rush'd from his work away.

But still through his life, when Hope held high
    Her cup full to the brim,
The demon whose life was his came by
    And dash'd the bliss from him.

Ah ! fearful story it was and seem'd
    To wear little purpose then ;
But its deeper truths have upon me gleam'd
    Since I look'd as a man on men.

SCOTT. 59

For still in the hurry and fret of life,
    When I see the brow bent down,
And the hand stretch'd out for the **straws of strife,**
    Instead of the golden crown,

Then I whisper—Here is one who moulds
    In his heart, and knows it not,
A monster that yet will burst its folds,
    And haunt him from **spot** to spot—

Haunt him till life's frail powers grow weak,
    And **the** hopes we keep **to** cheer
Turn away from the deathlike brow and cheek,
    And **come no more anear.**

Ah me ! what **wisdom this** might teach,
    If we lent but our ear and will ;
What inward things would rise up and preach,
    For our better **guidance** still !

But this working world rolls on, and we shape
    All things but the high divine ;
And still, far down in our heart, we ape
    The story of Frankenstein.

SCOTT.

OW thou to Genius, and thy worship **give**
    To our Magician, who, with wondrous wand,
    Walk'd through the realms of fiction's fairy land,
And bade the past in sweetest colours live :
Bow thou to him while ever luminous,
    Within thy **heart, sweet forms** upstart and say—
    We, **too,** will **worship at his** shrine this day,
For in him we have life, as he in us.
Hearing these voices that from boyhood's years
    Have kept **their friendship on** unchanged, canst thou
    Refuse thy **homage** to **their** master now,
Who through the halo of the past appears
    Simple, serene, and wise, and king alone
    Of realms a world's praise has made his own ?

THE STEERIN' WEE LADDIE.

HE winna sup his poshie, the buffy, curly loon,
But spurs and spurtles on my knee, an' quarrels for the spoon,
Rubbin' till his een grow red, and than anither yell ;
Oh, an awfu' plague's that laddie wha wants to sup himsel'.

See hoo he dauds the spoon away, as wud as wud can be,
Scalin' a' the sowp, an' lebbrin' baith himsel' an' me ;
Pushin' against the table wi' his wee shanks firm an' stieve,
Tryin' to sup wi' perfect spite his parritch wi' his nieve !

Weel, weel, be quate, for ony sake, I'll draw your wee chair in,
An' tie ye to the back, an' pit a cloot aneath your chin,
Gie ye the spoon into your han'—ye thrawn, ill-natured tyke !—
An' ye can try an' sup them, or dae wi' them what ye like.

Noo, since he's suppin' a' his lane, as quate as ony mouse,
I'll turn my back an' redd the floor, an' tidy up the house ;
For when he toddles up an' doon, he's sic a steerin' lim',
I canna get a han's wark dune for lookin' after him.

Losh me, what awfu' screigh is that ? I'll turn me roun' an' see :
He's cowpit ow'r the bowl, an' ramm'd the spoon-shank in his e'e ;
Then what a cry for mammy comes, that I maun let alane
What wark I had to dae, an' tak' him on my knee again.

Noo, whisht, my wee, wee mannie, ye've got an awfu' scaur,
But, gin your face an' han's were washed, ye're no a preen the waur ;
Noo, whisht, an' kiss your mammy, ye're no sae much to blame,
For mony an aulder ane than you has dune the very same.

Ay, mony a bearded man, atweel, has gane sae far ajee,
That ever after hung his head, nor cared to lift an e'e,
But slunk aboot, an' a' for what I brawly weel can tell :
He grew ow'r croose, an' far ow'r sune began to sup himsel'.

THE PREACHER.

THE spirit of God fell on him, and he pass'd
  From out the common bounds wherein we move,
And like a mantle round his life he cast
  The grandeur of his mission from above.

Yet his was no dull eye that look'd askance
  In scorn on daily human things, but bright
With all the beaming virtue of a glance
  That took its brightness from his Master's light.

He leant not unto narrow bound or goal,
  But in the wisdom of the teaching years
Grew up large-hearted with a yearning soul
  For all the faith in human love and tears.

Rough was his brow and cheek, but rougher still
  The hand you clasp'd, yet in its kindly heat
Was felt the endeavour, and the quiet will
  That walks through life with firm, unshaken feet.

He knew his mission, and like Paul he preach'd
  With throbbing lips, and eyes whose holy ire
Lit up at all that from of old hath teach'd
  The brute-like limit and the clay desire.

But when he knelt beside the dying bed
  Of some worn one to whom this world was naught,
Around him like celestial light he shed
  The love and mercy of the faith he taught.

Ah, how the features wore to placid peace,
  As in mute thankfulness that restless life
Should thus in such a golden vision cease,
  That but before was full of pain and strife.

This was the faith he held as best and first—
  The faith of heart and life ; the other still

Lay in all toil and labour, and the thirst
    Of science and her miracles of skill.

And these two in him ever living on,
    Made music, even as two chords that blend
Each into each, making a glorious tone
    That led his footsteps unto fruitful end.

The beggar came, and not in vain, to crave,
    And heard him whisper at his lowly door—
" The poor is always with you," and he gave
    With open hand a pittance from his store.

The very children left their innocent mirth
    In summer nights to sit upon his knee,
And hear him talk of all the brighter earth
    Above our own, and Christ he soon would see.

He sees him now ; for at His master's will,
    With spirit earnest, trusting, strong, and brave,
He pass'd into his endless rest ; and still
    The sexton points you out the preacher's grave.

MAGGIE'S WEAN.

I KEN'D Maggie weel ere she grew to a wife,
An' smiled in the sunshine o' a' its sweet life ;
But, wae's me, a twalmonth had scarce gane to rest
Ere the green kirkyard sod was laid ow'r her young breast,
Leavin' to this cauld warld, to warsle its lane,
A wee feeble lifie they ca'd Maggie's wean.

But it took root, and grew, for the angels abune
Water a' the buds left by their stems far ow'r sune,
Wi' their sweetest o' tears, that fa' saft as the dew,
While the mither looks on wi' a smile on her broo,
An' a fond half-hid yearning, that tells aye hoo fain
She wad come back ance mair to her mitherless wean.

But it thrived like a breckan fu' bonnie to see,
A canty bit thing fu' o' lauchin' an' glee ;
An' prood were they a' ow'r this waif frae the strife,
When the cauld wave o' death wreck'd a mither's sweet life ;
So ae afternoon a thocht enter'd my brain,
To gang up ance erran' an' see Maggie's wean.

When I gaed ben the room the wee lassie was there,
An' I scarce had got richt settled doon in the chair
Till she toddled up to me, and frankly and kin'
Put her wee han' sae trustfu' and saft into mine—
Lookin' up as if tryin' some thocht to explain,
Ken'd to nae ither body but Maggie's wee wean.

Then she lauch'd when we lauch'd, till in very delicht
Her pawkie blue een creepit fair oot o' sicht ;
Tum'led ow'r the least thing that took haud o' her tae,
Put a froon on her broo, then wi' smiles chase't away ;
Play'd her queerist o' tricks at a word ow'r again—
Nae winner her fowk's prood ow'r Maggie's wee wean.

Then she row'd wi' the dog on the rug a' her lane,
Her wee dumpy nose close to that o' his ain ;
An' aye as his braid sonsie lugs got a pu',
Or his rough sides a dunch frae her han' or her broo,
He look'd proodly roun', as if tellin' us plain
That nane got sic freedom but Maggie's wee wean.

What a changfu' bit creature, for aye noo an' than,
When she took to the dumps, an' her mou' got half-thrawn,
Losh me ! in a moment, afore ye could speak,
A sunny smile brichten'd her broo an' her cheek,
An' her blue een cam' oot like the skies after rain ;
She's the April o' mitherless tots—Maggie's wean.

An' I couldna but think, as we join'd in her glee,
If the mither had been but amang us to see
A' the turns an' the flichts o' her wee dawtie's mirth,
What a joy wad been hers, far abune a' on earth,
As she clappit an' cuddled, prood, smirkin', an' fain,
Her Lilliput sel' in her ain bonnie wean.

But I thocht, an' I think, that she still lookit doon
Frae her ain happy hame wi' the angels abune,
Whisperin' words to her bairnie we couldna hear said,
Layin' han's that we couldna see on her wee head,
While the bricht, happy smiles were but types o' her ain,
Fa'in' saft as her love on the broo o' her wean.

Ay me ! this auld warl' moves on wi' sic stride,
That the best o' oor thochts are flung a' to the side,
An' we think, as the soun' fills the braid toilin' day,
That alang wi't God draws Himsel' farrer away ;
But He speaks oot amang us at times unco plain,
When we look on a wee smilin' mitherless wean.

TO ONE IN ETERNITY.

" Nicht darf ich dir zu gleichen mich vermessen."—Goethe.

I KNOW not how to sing a song to-day—
Thou in the spirit, I within the clay.
Perchance it may be that these many years
In the wide universe of starry spheres
Have made thee all unfit to hear a strain
Sung by a mortal bound to mortal pain ;
Yet would I deem the link that thou and I
Wove in our heart may still all time defy,
And wake when touch'd with a fraternal glow—
Thou far above, and I on earth below.

I dare not lift my purblind faith to thine,
Nor deem thy thoughts may still companion mine ;
For I am yet of earthly things, but thou
Hast the eternal world upon thy brow,
And wearest in the glory of thine eyes
The hush and calm of the eternal skies,
While past and present and the things to be
Move from thy footsteps like a mighty sea,
And Love (another name for God) attends
Thy slightest wish, and like a rainbow bends

Clear and all radiant, since it hath no sin,
Above thy going out and coming in.
Methinks betimes that thou, so far above
The reach of human, though all-yearning love,
Hast naught in common with the things I seek,
Whose aims may place the blush upon thy cheek ;
But when the daylight flies the breath of night,
And all the stars are crowding into light,
I sink in dreams that make the shadows shine
And bring thy spirit nearer unto mine.
Then, lo ! I see thee, and again I trace
The cherish'd features of thy smiling face ;
Once more we wander gladly hand in hand
Far down the sunshine of the past's sweet land ;
Stand on the bank that girds the well-known lake,
And laugh to see the waves our shadows take ;
Then plunge into the waving woods to view
Each fairy spot our prying childhood knew ;
And I would clasp thee, for the summer day
Hath lifted up my soul, and I am gay.
But lo ! ye sink and fade away, as fades
On the far hills the warm sweet summer shades,
And I am left alone to wake, and creep
Back to my human nature but to weep.

There be at times when all my heart grows chill,
And shakes as if beneath some pending ill,
That all its wishes waken up, and grow
Restless for something which is not below,
But pure, and all ethereal as a star
New lit in the night heaven clear and far ;
Then think I in such moments, when I feel
These better glimpses o'er my being steal,
That it is thou, dear spirit, who on high
Still yearnest, with compassion in thine eye,
For thy frail link below, that yet remains
Bound to the rough, dull earth and all its pains—
So fain would lift me by thy faith and love
To all the sunshine crowning thee above.

How shall I reach thee ?   For, though wrapt in earth,
My aspirations claim a higher birth,

E

And yearn to mix with thine in that high clime
Where tears are never—neither death nor time.
Lo! that sweet faith which sprung from Him who came
To wear our human sympathy and name—
He who in Holy Land, 'mid many scorns,
Bore calmly on the cross His crown of thorns,
Then died that we might lean upon His might,
And be one with Him in eternal light.
Thus shall I reach thee; but, before I win
The higher bounds that keep thy spirit in,
I must wear out my pilgrimage of dust
In faith and love, and all the wider trust,
Knowing that many sorrows yet may come—
The fears that torture, doubts that speak though dumb,
Night-whisper'd yearnings, vain regrets, that gush
At strangely-chosen times, and the fond wish
That turns to gather what was bright and fair
In thy young life before the seal was there.
I will be patient, then, and with firm mind
Work out this life of mine, nor look behind,
Save but to gather strength from what I see
Of all the truth and love which was in thee,
Keeping such still within me as a trust
To lift me unto thee beyond the dust;
For I shall see thee, and this hope at last,
Falls balm-like on the sorrows that have past.
And, lo! the future widens out to me,
With all its pathways leading up to thee;
And so I bless thee till my very tears
Form rainbows brighter than when Summer rears
Her glistening clouds, and all the glory giv'n
Is but a link between this earth and heav'n,
Prone at its base I fall and bow my head,
As if in waiting for thy coming tread;
Then, when my heart is fit to be the guest,
For one short moment, of thy happy rest,
Pour down thy latest blessing upon me,
As from this earth I lift mine unto me.

THE FIRST PRIMROSE.

I STOOD within a wood, and heard the wind
   Keep up its music in the solemn trees,
But this could soothe me not, for in my mind
   My thoughts were ill **at ease** ;

And all day long had kept a questioning,
   Whose inward whispers fill'd **my breast with pain** ;
Then thought I, solitude will surely **bring**
   My quiet back again.

So forth into the **wood I went,** and there,
   With the sweet **things** that grew up fresh and green,
I tried to frame my thoughts, but a despair
   Came ever up between.

Then, full of bitterness, I turn'd to trace
   My homeward path, when, lo ! in golden hue
And smiling proudly from its secret place,
   A primrose met my view :

One primrose, with its **eye so** round and clear,
   That I leapt up as one for joy will sing,
And cried, "Though all this day be gloom, yet here
   Is one sweet trace of spring."

Therefore, **I** err'd when, in **my fear** and **doubt,**
   I wrapp'd myself in murmurs but **to miss**
Those placid breathing things, whose looks devout
   Still whisper to me this :

Mortal, that will **not look in** trust beyond
   The mist and darkness of this life, and see
How all points ever to the one great bond
   Between thy God and thee.

Look up, and if the sky be dull and **dark,**
   The blue is still above, whose **sunny scope**

E 2

Is all-eternal with the glorious spark
  That lights the lamp of hope.

Then weary not, but gird thyself with strength,
  From ever mute but potent preachers drawn,
Who, in their change and bloom, but point at length
  One universal dawn.

THE ENGINE.

On fire-horses and wind-horses we career.—*Carlyle.*

HURRAH! for the mighty engine,
  As he bounds along his track :
Hurrah, for the life that is in him,
  And his breath so thick and black ;
And hurrah for our fellows, who in their need
  Could fashion a thing like him—
With a heart of fire, and a soul of steel,
  And a Samson in every limb.

Ho, stand from that narrow path of his,
  Lest his gleaming muscles smite,
Like the flaming sword the archangel drew
  When Eden lay wrapp'd in night ;
For he cares, not he, for a paltry life
  As he rushes along to the goal,
It but costs him a shake of his iron limb,
  And a shriek from his mighty soul.

Yet I glory to think that I help to keep
  His footsteps a little in place,
And he thunders his thanks as he rushes on
  In the lightning speed of his race ;
And I think that he knows when he looks at me,
  That, though made of clay as I stand,
I could make him as weak as a three hours' child
  With a paltry twitch of my hand.

But I trust in his strength, and he trusts in me,
    Though made but of brittle clay,
While he is bound up in the toughest of steel,
    That tires not night or day ;
But for ever flashes, and stretches, and strives,
    While he shrieks in his smoky glee—
Hurrah for the puppets that, lost in their thoughts,
    Could rub the lamp for me !

O, that some grand old Roman—
    Some quick, light Greek or two—
Could come from their graves for one half hour
    To see what my fellows can do ;
I would take them with me on this world's steed,
    And give him a little rein;
Then rush with his clanking hoofs through space,
    With a wreath of smoke for his mane.

I would say to them, as they shook in their fear,
    " Now what is your paltry book,
Or the Phidian touch of the chisel's point,
    That can make the marble look,
To this monster of ours, that for ages lay
    In the depths of the dreaming earth,
Till we brought him out with a cheer and a shout,
    And we hammer'd him into birth."

Clank, clank went the hammer in dusty shops,
    The forge flare went to the sky,
While still, like the monster of Frankenstein's,
    This great wild being was nigh ;
Till at length he rose up in his sinew and strength,
    And our fellows could see with pride
Their grimy brows and their bare, slight arms,
    In the depths of his glancing side.

Then there rose to their lips a dread question of fear—
    " Who has in him the nerve to start
In this mass a soul that will shake and roll
    A river of life to his heart ?"
Then a pigmy by jerks went up his side,
    Flung a globe of fire in his breast,

And cities leapt nearer by hundreds of miles
  At the first wild snort from his chest.

Then away he rush'd to his mission of toil,
  Wherever lay guiding rods,
And the work he could do at each throb of his pulse
  Flung a blush on the face of the gods.
And Atlas himself, when he felt his weight,
  Bent lower his quaking limb,
Then shook himself free from this earth, and left
  The grand old planet to him.

But well can he bear it, this Titan of toil,
  When his pathway yields to his tread ;
And the vigour within him flares up to its height,
  Till the smoke of his breath grows red ;
Then he shrieks in delight, as an athlete might,
  When he reaches his wild desire,
And from head to heel, through each muscle of steel,
  Runs the cunning and clasp of the fire.

Or, see how he shakes aside the night,
  And roars in his thirsty wrath,
While his one great eye gleams white with rage
  At the darkness that muffles his path ;
And lo ! as the pent-up flame of his heart
  Flashes out from behind its bars,
It gleams like a bolt flung from heaven, and rears
  A ladder of light to the stars.

Talk of the sea flung back in its wrath
  By a line of unyielding stone,
Or the slender clutch of a thread-like bridge,
  That knits two valleys in one !
Talk of your miracle-working wires,
  And their world-embracing force,
But *himmel !* give me the bits of steel,
  In the mouth of the thunder-horse !

Ay, give me the beat of his fire-fed breast,
  And the shake of his giant frame,

And the sinews that work like the shoulders of Jove
    When he launches a bolt of flame ;
And give me that Lilliput rider of his,
    Stout and wiry and grim,
Who can vault on his back as he puffs his pipe,
    And whisk the breath from him.

Then hurrah for our mighty engine, boys ;
    He may roar and fume along
For a hundred years ere a poet arise
    To shrine him in worthy song ;
Yet if one with the touch of the gods on his lips,
    And his heart beating wildly and quick,
Should rush into song at this demon of ours,
    Let him sing, too, the shovel and pick.

OOR RAB.

OOR Rab's in his bed, an' he's sleepin' sae soun'
That afore he wad wauken the hoose micht fa' doon.
 Sae I'll juist steer the fire up an' mak' some repair
On his troosers, an' cover his hurdies ance mair ;
For, as fack as I'm leevin', I thocht perfect shame,
When an' auld neebor lass cam' to see my snug hame,
When he bang'd in amang us, demandin' a piece,
His rags hingin' down like a half-cuisten fleece.

But ane needna think ony shame o' their ain,
Though nae mither wi' han's could keep claes on sic wean,
For frae mornin' till nicht there's nae rest for his feet,
But a constant rin on till I'm weary tae see't.
Na, when suppin' his parritch at nicht I declare
He keeps thumpin' on wi' his heels on the fluir.
It's a wunner to me that I hae wi' hale banes
This wee wan'rin' Jew o' a' ill-steerin' weans.

Then what wark he has makin' wee boats that maun soom,
Though the last ane he made he near sniggit his thoom ;

An' braw paper mills to whirl roun' wi' the wun',
When set oot on the knowe wi' their shanks in the grun',
Forbye ither things I micht coont by the score
That he mak's oot o' sticks that lie bing'd at the door.
'Deed, his faither himsel' wunners hoo he can mak'
Siccan things—he's a perfect mechanic, in fack.

But wae tae that day when the sodgers cam' roun',
An' gaed fifin' an' prancin' like mad through the toon ;
For months after that a' the auld broken boards
That his hands got a haud o' he turn'd into swords,
An' gaed stoggin' aboot in his sodger-like pride,
Wi' ane near as lang as himsel' at ilk side.
Losh, I laucht, till I scarce could draw yairn through a sock,
At the way he could mimic the red-coated folk.

But it cam' tae an en' wi' the wee warlike fule,
For ridin' ae day on the lang-leggit stule,
The big, braid-croon'd bonnet o' braw tartan claith,
That his faither got made when the chaps play'd Macbeth,
Gaed clean ow'r his een, and it blin'd him sae sair,
That he fell wi' his heid 'gainst the edge o' a chair.
But I thocht as I cuddled the wee sabbin' limb,
A' wha gie wark for sodgers should tum'le like him.

Yet he's no ill ava', though at times, dae ye see,
He raises curmurs 'tween his faither an' me,
For he cries when he happens to hear o' his tricks,
" Wi', as fack as ocht, Jean, ye should gi'e him his licks."
But I say to him, " John, what's the use o' this rage,
The bairn's nae wheet waur than the rest at his age ;"
An' the rogue (for he kens that he's dear to my heart)
Pu's my goon a' the while that I'm takin' his pairt.

I like my bit bairnie, an' whiles as I shoo,
I big up air-castles tae please my ain view ;
Then I see him grown up buirdly, sonsie, an' braw,
The prop o' oor age, an' the pride o' us a' ;
Nae draighlin' wi' horses, and stannin' the brash
O' the cauld winter day, but a job wi' some cash,
An' aye a guid coat that he buttons, instead
O' flingin't clean aff him tae win his bit bread.

Nae doot but I'm wrang tae look ow'r far afore,
Though somehow I think that a' this is in store,
An' aften my heart gi'es a loup as I think
Hoo the neebors will say, " Fegs, her lad's nae sma' drink."
I say this tae John, but he turns unco snell,
Though I ken a' the time that he thinks sae himsel'.
Lod, wha kens but some heiress may think him a grab,
When we ca' him oor Robert, instead o' oor Rab.

THE BRIDGE.

I WENT to-night by the wooden bridge
    That steps across the stream ;
And I leant a little over its ledge
    To take a half-hour's dream.

For sweetly to their depths were stirr'd
    Our hearts two nights ago,
When she and I stood still and heard
    The stream sing on below.

But all was changed and cold to me,
    The charm had fled away ;
The light that lit up hill and tree
    Had lost its old display.

And yet the moon was in the sky,
    The stream sang sweet and clear ;
Now, heart, canst thou not tell me why
    I held that night so dear ?

Was it that she beside me stood,
    Like some one from above,
And sent through all my rougher mood
    The gentleness of love ?

Or that mine eyes partook the tone
    Of hers, and saw the earth
Like one great book wide open thrown
    Beneath a better birth ?

To this my heart would not reply,
 Nor speak its thoughts to me ;
And still the stream and field and sky
 Grew strange and cold to see.

Now what, I question'd still, can bring
 The old look back again,
And place as in a fairy ring
 This spot, and still my pain.

Then some sweet spirit in the air,
 Whose mission is to move
Around young bosoms, heard my pray'r,
 And whisper'd " One you love."

O sudden voice of sweet surprise,
 What truth is in thy tone,
That two can find a paradise
 Where one—but gloom alone.

Thine, then, was all the light and bliss
 That made that night so dear ;
Come ! wake me with thy sweetest kiss,
 And let thy soul be here.

Vain wish ! yet strange that two sweet eyes
 And brow and neck of snow
Could make the moon within the skies
 Pour down her softest glow ;

And stranger still one form held dear,
 Standing beside my own,
Had pow'r to make the stream so clear,
 And sing with such a tone.

THE WIND BLOWS SOFT.

THE wind blows soft, and cool, and sweet,
 As it blew in my infancy ;
And as leaves burst out when their juice grows sweet,
 So my thoughts rise up in me.

And again, with my bosom beating high,
   I enter my boyhood land,
While the dreams that fade but can never die,
   Come and take me by the hand ;

And they lead me away from my daily thought,
   Then leave me as whispers die,
Lying all alone in some fairy spot,
   Looking up to the summer sky.

And the sunlight, as soft as a maiden's breath,
   Comes cool through the leaves above,
And lights on my brow with a steadfast faith,
   And an all-unchanging love.

Ah ! thus it fell in the long ago,
   When my heart beat firm and strong,
And my spirit leapt up with its brightest glow,
   At the first sweet breath of song.

Then there fell a light on field and hill ;
   But that light has lost its glow,
Yet my heart at times feels its sweetness still,
   As I feel the sunlight now;

And from out that sweetness comes and goes,
   Like the gush of summer springs,
The music that trembles within, and flows
   From the sunshine of vanish'd things.

And through all my life, as I work away,
   That music follows me—
Speaking out, in the pauses of the day,
   In many a melody.

Thus it comes that my heart still keeps its prime,
   And, when sunlight is sweet and strong,
Dreams itself away to that boyhood time, -
   And its first wild gush of song.

DANTE.

BRIGHTLY shone the brow of Dante,
    In those years of early youth,
When his Beatrice, like an angel,
    Rose before him in her truth.

And he sang in happy music,
    All the beauty that she bore—
Sang her maiden truth and sweetness—
    Made her famous evermore.

In that golden time what worship
    Rang with most melodious chime
From his inmost haunt of being,
    Making all his life sublime.

Cool and sweet was then the laurel,
    Clasping his unfurrow'd brow,
Glowing with the future gladness,
    And the lover's faith and vow.

Thus I like to think of Dante,
    As he stept in light along ;
Worshipping in golden visions,
    She who came and woke his song.

But I turn away in sadness
    From the pain, and gloom, and tears,
Rising upward with that vision,
    In the midway of his years :

Turn away from all its shadows,
    To that first sweet spring of song,
When his Beatrice starr'd his youthtime,
    And his soul had felt no wrong.

W I L L I E .

H E'S a deil o' **a wean**—what ava can he mean ?
   Lod, he'll ow'r-gang us **a'** yet, an' that'll be seen ;
   Here's his **spleet-new** bit pony left **on the** door **stane**,
The heid **chow'd** away, an' twa legs o' it gane ;
An' **a'** just because it got into his heid
He'd hae ane like the baker's that comes wi' the **breid**.
Sic a wasterfu' callan'—I firmly believe
That the bump 'hint his lug is as big as my neive.

He first got a **barrow to** whurl up an' doon,
An' for days after that he **was through the hale toon ;**
He push'd it wheel first **up** the steps **o' the** stairs,
He whurl'd it alang a' the **taps o'** the chairs,
He squeez'd it through a' the strait neuks he could get,
An' when it stuck fast **he flew into** a pet.
Na, when a' roun' the fire when the forenichts **were snell,**
He aye made a place for't alang wi' himsel'.

But ae afternoon, an' a gude laugh I had,
He grat to hae't through 'tween the legs o' **his dad ;**
An' his faither, the sulks like a clud on **his broo**,
Had to **striddle an'** let the wee sorra whirl't through.
An' lang **did he** lauch ow'r the trick he had dune,
But an hour after that he was changin' his tune,
For the barrow—an' anxious an' lang did he try—
Wadna **break**, sae he flung't **on the coal-knowe oot-bye.**

He next got a hammer, but that was faur **waur,**
For the first day he knockit a knob aff the **draw'r ;**
The second, he crackit my auld favourite jug,
An' for that, when I gied him **a** dawd on the lug,
He up wi' the **hammer, but** sic was his speed,
That in tryin' to hit me he struck his ain heid,
Sae he sat doon, an' after he'd grat his desire,
Flung the hammer **to** burn at the back o' the fire.

But yesterday, juist, when some faut he could help
Gar't me turn up his hurdies and gie them a skelp,

The dour look cam' down, while he keepit his place,
An', "Dang ye," he said, lookin' up in my face;
Losh ! my heart gied a loup, for fu' weel did I ken
What he ettled to say had nae "g" at the en';
Still, I dinna ken hoo he could come by sic word,
For his faither's nae swearer that ever I heard.

I never said wrang was the word he had sain,
For I ken'd it wad just make him say't ow'r again,
But that nicht when he bedded, an' lay like a tap,
An' I sat by the fire wi' his claes in my lap,
I whisper'd tae John in a lown kind o' way,
"Dae ye ken what wee Willie cam' oot wi' the day ?"
Sae I tell'd him, but a' that I got was juist " Tat,
Aulder anes than oor bairn hae a fashion o' that."

He's a droll wean ava, though, an speaks wi' a twang,
An' like some muirlan' herd has a swag wi' his gang;
Then sae sleeky an' slid when he lays oot his traps
For bawbees to buy candie, aiples, an' snaps;
An' sae sweet wi' the tongue, here's the way he comes on—
" Eh, but mither, you're bonnie, gie's some curran' scone."
Fegs, when ance he grows up he'll mak' some lassie's e'e
Brichten up like my ain when John pookit at me.

But whiles when I'm sittin' an' thinkin' my lane
I fin' that we're far waur to blame than the wean;
For ye see, when the neebors at nicht daun'er in,
We canna but tell what the callan' has dune;
An' they lauch an' we lauch, while the rogue a' the while
(Though the dirt on his face micht weel cover his smile)
Keeks roun' him sae bardy, then turns his bit back,
Prood, nae doot, at his bein' the hale o' oor crack.

He'll men' though, when ance he grows up an' has mense,
For ye canna expect him to hae muckle sense,
An' weel-behaved weans, wi' their mim, solemn looks,
Are naewhere fa'n in wi' save in bits o' books;
But wha kens, when he comes to be buirdly an' douce,
Wi' his wage comin' in every week to the hoose,
That we'll say to the neebors, wha speak in his praise,
Quate? " Dear me, the callan was that a' his days."

THE VILLAGE FIDDLER.

I SEE him yet, that **grey** old man,
    Whose fiddle made many a winter night
Pass by **as** only **fiddlers** can,
    With reels and jigs as swift as light ;
I see him still, **as** if to-day
    He sat beside me, hale and strong,
And question'd, " What am **I** to play ?"
    And **drew** the bow the strings along.

He sits **within his** elbow **chair,**
    The fiddle laid across his **knee ;**
He runs his **fingers** through **his hair,**
    And quaintly asks, " What news **may be ?"**
He takes a snuff ; **the** box careers
    Around us, **till the** powder speaks,
And we must bow to feel the tears
    Make mimic Derbies down **our cheeks.**

He tells **us many a** jest the while
    His small blue sparkling eye peeps out,
And the **dry** shadow of a smile
    Plays all his pucker'd **cheek about ;**
Quaint stories of the olden times,
    And quips, and humours, without **end,**
All dress'd **up** as **I** dress my rhymes
    Before **I** send them to the *Friend.*

He takes the fiddle up, he brings
    Each **tone to** its most perfect part ;
He lays the bow along the strings,
    And his whole soul is in his art ;
He plays, with all his skill and show,
    Our favourite reels and dear strathspeys,
Then gives a flourish with the bow,
    And looks around to claim our praise.

Ah, heart ! but he shall play no more,
    And the old light has left our touch,

Or I should tempt the Stygian shore,
   And draw him from King Pluto's clutch ;
For others here who scrape and chime
   Are only fit to make me sick—
Dull fools, who, using Jeffrey's rhyme,
   "Move nothing but their fiddlestick."

Well, well ; we miss him from the street,
   And in our coming nights of mirth
No more his fiddle, brisk and sweet,
   Shall draw us to his silent hearth.
Yet rest his dust ; and we behind,
   Who yet in fancy hear him play,
May pause at times, and call to mind
   The village Orpheus pass'd away.

THE POET—A DREAM.

A BREATH went through the Universe, and shook
   All things to music, and a mighty voice
Roll'd upward like a psalm, and whisper'd, "Take
The task of poet, and be half a god."

Then soft, as when an angel's folding wing
Stirs the rich calm of Paradise, a power
Came in upon me, and my heart grew warm,
And I became a poet, and was crown'd.

Then life rose up to myriad forms of use,
And love was at the birth of each ; and I,
Who look'd not with the look of common men,
But with far other vision, sang their faiths
To cheer my fellows—not in songs of dim
And cunning music, but all high and clear,
As fit for toiling lips ; for so the gods
Had will'd it when their shadows fell on me.
I sang the world, with its burst of thought
And ever-toiling sinews, in whose strength
Lay hid those miracles that yet would be

When Time from out the years would raise his hand,
And bid them spread **their** wonders.   Then I touch'd
The coming splendour **of a** brotherhood
Wide **as the** sunlight, 'neath whose radiance men
Would **cry for** fellowship, and fight with hate
And **envy, and from** out the world's great fields
Root **war for ever,** and within their soil
Plant peace and harvests waving wide for all.
I went with Science and her giant **train**
Of Titan working things, and I became
Firm in their strength, and taught **it to my** kind
As best, but Labour next (for Labour **still**
Is the true crown of manhood), and **I link'd**
To such brown dignity the noblest **use**
That hearts can rise to when their pulses beat
With love and wisdom.   Thus **I sang, and as**
The years came onward, still within me grew
The power of words, whose cunning, **spreading** out,
Made me an empire in the human breast,
And **in** all climes and tongues, and I became
Firm in **my task** and office, till at last
A voice rose from the latest of my years—
" The mission finish'd, all the grosser dies,
And rounds to **dust** and ashes."   Then methought
The mould of clay shrunk from my purer shape,
And I was free in space ; but, as I paused
Half-way to heaven, with all the gods in view,
And the cool laurel on my brow, I turn'd,
And gave my spirit to my fellow-men.

THE MAY.

" Du Wonne der Natur."—Schiller

COME away **to** the woodland bowers,
  Where the **shade** is soft and sweet,
 And pillow the head on the first bright flowers
  Where the angels have set their feet ;
 And there, while every breathing thing
  Bids the spirit of **ours** be gay,

Let us lift as with one voice and sing
  A welcome to the May.

    O the May, the May, the May,
    The bright and sunny May!
    If this life of mine is bound to be
    A life of constant toil to me,
    Let me lighten it with the May.

The primrose blooms wherever a rill
  Gives music to the dell;
The violet peeps with fair good will
  Beside the mossy well;
The birds leap out in joyous throngs
  From the snowy hawthorn spray,
And stir the air with a thousand songs
  In honour of the May.

The gentle clouds within the sky
  Beseem a silver mass,
Whose shadows glide all softly by
  Upon the daisied grass;
And when their fleecy richness parts,
  The blue peeps out all gay,
So come and let us fill our hearts
  With the wisdom of the May.

I would not waste one single thought
  On the sour and bigot breast,
That points out heaven as its lot,
  And gloom for all the rest;
Whose lip with hate and scorn can part,
  But may no smile display,
And wears deep down in the dull dim heart
  December instead of May.

O, if at times within thy soul
  A bitterness arise,
And restless thoughts that fix their goal
  In gloom before thine eyes,
Look round you in an hour like this
  And all will flee away,

And leave behind a better mind,
    And the beauty of the May.

What though our lot be lowly set
    In labour's brotherhood?
Stand up, and fling away regret,
    The world is wise and good.
Work! this is life's eternal task
    That all have to obey,
And duty done is but the sun
    That gives this life a May.

If on this head of mine should light
    The snowy hue of years,
Still may this earth have to my sight
    The look which now it wears;
So that, if pain and care should smart
    The twilight of decay,
Let us ever have within our heart
    The light and warmth of May.

Then come away to the woodland bowers,
    Where the stream is swift and strong,
And, if other hearts be sad, let ours
    This day exult in song.
Why, 'twere a shame to the brow that wears
    Its world-look to-day,
And the heart that still will hoard its cares,
    And this the month of May.

            O the May, the May, the May,
                The bright and sunny May!
            If this life of mine is bound to be
            A life of constant toil to me,
                Let me lighten it with the May.

ARTEMUS WARD.

I LIKE Artemus Ward, that quaint
 Rough, sturdy, antiquated Showman,
Who travell'd Yankee-land to paint
 The social ills in man and woman ;
Who when he found some growing vice
 In need of moral exhibition,
Threw out his handbills in a trice,
 And drew his show into position ;

Then ground his organ with a smile
 Of humour on his comic features,
As he prepared himself the while
 To edify misguided creatures ;
Who, when some happy " goak" escaped,
 That made them gape and grin like niggers,
Together fifteen cents they scraped,
 And hurried in to see his " figgers."

I like his style, so rich and rife
 With that delicious chaff and banter,
That tickles up your inward life,
 And pricks your spirit to a canter :
Quaint sayings, oddly said yet trite,
 And maxims peeping from their dwelling
Of words made shorter to the sight
 By quips of most eccentric spelling.

What cared he how he wrote or spell'd,
 Or shorten'd diphthongs in their stature ?
The nicer rules were to be held
 As checks on his nomadic nature.
A foe to other tame pursuits,
 He lived but in his pet direction
Of " moril snaiks" and " wax statoots,"
 For fallen man's minute inspection.

He had his pride, too, in his way,
 And liked his own opinion vastly,

And chuckled when he could display
   Some sparkling " eppygram" in—lastly.
Nor cared he for a scrape or two—
   For such things made him turn adviser,
And place them in a comic view,
   To make his tickled reader wiser.

So when I lift him from the shelf
   To read—although I own that no man
Has less of fancy than myself—
   At once before me stands the Showman.
I listen to his "goaks," and find
   That I, made mellow with his chaffing,
Must bless the Molière of his kind,
   And make his panegyric laughing.

A LEGEND OF ST PATRICK.

I HEARD this old legend a few days ago—
   A legend so quaint
   Of Ireland's saint,
   That to lighten my time
   I have put it in rhyme,
Just to see how it looks with the lines all a-row.

When St Patrick, that worthy dear man, came to see
How the reptiles polluted his darling " conthree,"
He determined to stamp them, so set out with glee
To hunt them with curses until they should flee
To less favour'd nations over the sea,
   Where they might rest their feet,
   ·Safe in some snug retreat,
And have leisure to cool themselves down from their heat,
And make moral reflections on life being sweet.

Well, he made short work with the most of their tribe,
By cajoling, coaxing, and tipping a bribe ;
But the serpent, so cunning and sly from the first,
Was a tickler, and puzzled St Patrick the worst ;

He was firm as the granite, and wouldn't give in,
Though he shook right before him a purse full of tin.
      No, no,
      He wouldn't go ;
And he swore an oath he might change his skin
If his conscience permitted the tempter to win.

Now, St Patrick was fairly nonpluss'd, nor could tell
What to do with this reptile, so cunning and fell ;
At length, to his infinite joy and delight,
He hit on a plan to put matters right ;
        So he got a box,
        And began to coax,
As he open'd the lid with a confident air,
Like a country packman displaying his ware,
And, " Look here," cried he, " what a place to hold
Your delicate form, and no fear of the cold ;
Here you'll lie through the night-time as snug as paint ;
And I pledge you my faith and my truth as a saint
That as soon as the cock hails the morn with a shout
I'll rise up with the lark and I'll let you out."

        But the serpent was sly,
        So he shut one eye,
As he said, with a half-incredulous sigh,
" But really, St Patrick, the box is too small,
And I don't think it ever would hold me at all ;
Let me see it again.   O, no, I defy it."
Said St Patrick blandly, " Just you try it ;
        And if it won't do,
        Why, between us two,
You can creep out again, and no harm will ensue."

Now the serpent, to prove that St Patrick was wrong
(And saints step aside, or there's no truth in song),
Slipp'd into the box, slowly packing himself
Neat as garments new folded and laid on a shelf,
Till at last, when no more of his bulk could get in,
A foot of his tail was left squirming without,
So he cried, with a grin, " Patrick, dear, do you doubt ?"
But the Saint was his match, and " Look out for your skin !"

He thunder'd ; and down came the lid with a crash ;
But his serpentship, seeing no end to the smash,
Drew his tail in as quick as the lightning's flash,
And was box'd at last, safe as miser's cash.

Then St Patrick took up the box, and away
He went to some lake or inland bay,
Whose name the legend forgets to say ;
There he flung it in, and it sank like the sword
That Lancelot threw to save that of his lord.
(See Tennyson's poem ; " Morte d'Arthur's" the name.)
More my Muse will not say, as her flights are but tame :
Besides, being anxious to finish this rhyme,
She looks right ahead, as if working on time.

Well, to finish my story.   Strange to say,
Whenever you happen to go by that way,
And you pause by that spot where St Patrick gave
That wily old " varmint" a watery grave,
You can hear him still, if you use your ear,
   As he squirms about in a restless fret,
Crying out, through the waters, loud and clear,
   " Sure, St Patrick, is it not morning yet ?"

MORAL.

Now for a moral ; and morals are sweet,
If they're dish'd up to you with their number of feet.
When the Devil proposes a nice little treat,
And smiles on you blandly to hide his deceit,
And you feel in your bosom your conscience repeat
Nice maxims you care not about in your heat,
But rely on your wisdom, and think it complete ;
If he gets in your head, then farewell to your feet.

HOPE AND SLEEP.

FROM THE FRENCH OF VOLTAIRE.

Du dieu qui nous créa la clémence infinie,
Pour adoucir, &c.

THE God who made us in infinite pow'r,
To cheer the woes of life's uncertain hour,
Has placed amongst us two of such sweet birth
That never brighter dwellers were on earth.
Solace in toils, in pain and care a prop,
One is sweet Slumber, and the other Hope.
One, when man, weaken'd, feels his frame at length
Shorn of its vigour and embracing strength,
Comes with calm pace, and pours his soothing ray,
And all his pains in slumber pass away.
The other fires our heart, inspires our will,
And even when cheating gives true pleasure still;
But to those favour'd ones on whom her dews
Are pour'd by heaven no fleeting joy ensues,
For fresh from God she brings His strength and stay,
Pure even as He—so endless is her sway.

BLIND ELLA.

" O, eine edle Himmelsgabe ist
Das licht des auges."—*Schiller.*

OUR little Ella, with her love and light,
Made our sweet home a happy paradise,
Till all at once a shadow rose to blight
The deep blue lustre of her laughing eyes.

Slow, slow it came, still widening its abode,
But slower still the truth grew on our mind,
Till, after one heart-prayer to our God,
We woke, and found our little darling blind.

Then what deep pain was daily ours to see
   Those eyes, that were so large and full and sweet,
Turn blank and dim, nor light with childish glee
   To hear, at night, the coming of our feet.

She did not murmur, though her lips would grieve
   And question still, in all their silent pain,
" When shall this darkness go away, and leave
   The sunshine, and the long, broad fields again ?"

This pass'd away through time, and then she took,
   By turns, strange snatches of her former mirth,
And her face brighten'd, not with the old look,
   But bright enough to cheer our sadden'd hearth.

Her footsteps, hush'd for many a weary day,
   Began to stir, and round the little room
She patter'd, feeling her uncertain way,
   With tiny hands before her in the gloom.

Then, when it grew familiar to her tread,
   She ventured out, and by the lowly door
Sat, with the sunshine falling on her head
   From the blue skies that she would see no more.

Or, if her sisters brought her flowers, whose breath
   Told of the wood and meadow, she would smile,
And weave them into some fantastic wreath,
   Guessing their colours as she wove the while.

Then, when she finish'd, she would rise and trace
   Her way back to her seat upon our knee,
Present the flowers, and look up to our face
   As if those dear blind eyes of hers could see.

And, sitting there in quiet all alone,
   Dread thoughts within our breast would whisper still,
" Hast thou a future shaped for thy blind one ?"
   And then with sudden tears our eyes would fill.

God's ways are best, nor know we how He leads
   Our spirit unto His : the woes He sends

May seem in His large eyes but **golden threads**
  To lead us gently back to holier ends.

So **when** we lay our darling down to rest,
  And by her little bedside bow to pray,
He so works with His love within our breast
  That all our doubts and shadows flee away.

And lo, within the future's sunny scope,
  Our little Ella, **our** blind darling, stands,
And by her side an angel, bright as hope,
  Leading **her ever on** with sister hands.

A TERPSICHOREAN RECOLLECTION.

I TOOK her down a country dance,
  And ever in its giddy wheeling
Her eyes beam'd forth **the sweetest glance**
  That ever sent a poet reeling—
Dear **eyes**, within whose light I saw
  The cherub angel's golden riddle;
I listen'd to its tender law,
  And turn'd my back upon the **fiddle.**

How **I got** down that **heavenly row**
  Of **snowy skirts and** smiling **faces**
I know **not, nor can** Cupid know,
  Though held an **adept** in such cases.
I moved like some somnambulist,
  But still in all the maze forgetting
No point of clasp and turn and twist,
  And graceful whirl of pirouetting.

At length the dance was o'er, and I,
  No longer **bound to** music's measure,
Had time to clasp **her** hand and sigh,
  And whisper **to her** all my pleasure.
I breath'd into her willing ear,
  While still the blush would rise and hover,

Nonsense for older heads to hear,
  But highest wisdom to a lover.

I whisper'd of that wish'd-for time
  When Love, with all his sweet caressings,
Would pour, with many a merry chime,
  Upon our brows his choicest blessings.
And still her cheek took deeper glow,
  And still her eyes gave sweeter glances,
Till—strange, in half an hour or so,
  I smiled at all my built-up fancies.

For what with reels and other things,
  Each with the like result attended,
And Cupid drawing in his wings,
  I found my charmer grow less splendid—
In fact, I thought her very plain,
  And wonder'd how the deuce a passion
Could e'er have seized my heart and brain,
  Unless I wish'd to keep the fashion.

"Cui bono," thus at times I cry,
  That I should keep a heart so fickle,
That, seeing some sweet lip and eye,
  Must needs its luckless owner tickle.
But if such fate be laid as tax
  On those that ope the Muse's portals,
Then with some proser " I go snacks,"
  And link myself to sober mortals.

LAME KATIE.

LITTLE lame Katie, with her golden hair,
  And her dead mother's eyes, comes in to me,
Lays with a smile her crutch beside my chair,
  Then shakes her curls and climbs up to my knee ;

And as she sits, again I hear the tread
  Of her, the spirit now sainted and divine,

Who walk'd with me a space, then bow'd her head,
  Leaving this little life to cling to mine :

A tiny weight, yet hard, in truth, to bear
  When left to strive without a mate alone ;
Yet there was something that kept back despair
  When I look'd into eyes so like her own.

I did my best to nurse the helpless thing,
  And often, in my wish to make her smile,
Would I begin some old, sweet song to sing,
  The warm tears gushing to my eyes the while.

But when she grew up, and could use her crutch
  And run about, a load fell from my mind,
And lighter grew my task, though there was much
  Still left for earnest thought and care behind.

But we were happy, and at night our hearth
  Brighten'd with many a frolic between us two,
And God knows but my little cripple's mirth
  Went to my heart as soft as summer dew.

The children, too, at times would come and say,
  Looking up with their faces round and sweet,
" Katie must come with us to see us play,
  Just by the corner, further down the street."

Then, as she fetch'd her crutch, I turn'd about
  And wrapp'd her snugly in her little shawl,
Kiss'd her, and off they went with leap and shout,
  My poor dwarf'd thing the happiest of them all.

I, too, would often stand, unseen, to hear
  Their merry laughter, and my heart would bound
When Katie's rose up, soft, and sweet, and clear—
  Her mother's voice in bud in all its sound.

Then, when she came in, she would tell me all—
  How Jane had placed her in the ring, and then
How Mary toss'd, and how she caught the ball,
  Till in her prattle I grew young again.

So my rough being chords with her, but still,
　When twilight darkens down, within my breast
The old wound opens up against my will,
　When I lay my lame darling into rest.

But when I bow my head to hear her pray,
　I know that near a spirit mother stands
Unseen, yet bright from realms of endless day,
　Blessing us both with radiant lips and hands.

And so I dry my tears, and thank the love
　That still has left this little link behind,
Daily to grow in strength, till far above
　We walk in God's own light that will not blind.

THE FALLING LEAVES.

AH ! why will my heart beat faint and low
　At the sound of the falling leaves ?
And why do I turn to the long ago
　With the thoughts of one who grieves ?

Is it that the dreams that once were mine,
　In the years when hope was rife,
Have fallen each from their high design,
　And rot in a vanish'd life ?—

Wither and rot in the silent dust,
　As the dead in the churchyards do ;
And all unseen, till some thought's quick gust
　Whirls their skeletons up to view ?

And still as my heart would own this truth,
　The falling leaves would say
They were dreams of a hot and fickle youth,
　And could not but pass away.

But thy manhood now must have healthier strife,
　And hopes of higher beams,

And more of work in thy daily life,
   And less of the early dreams.

For the future is not for he who yearns
   For the vanish'd and useless past;
But for he who strives onward still, nor turns,
   But battles to the last.

Go thou, then, into thy life, nor sigh
   For the dreams that have **sunk and fled**;
But knit thyself to the hopes **that die,**
   But to blossom overhead.

For we, too, go to the silent earth,
   In the dirge **of the** Autumn rain;
But even our fall has a sound of mirth,
   For we know we shall come again:

Come in the glow and the flush of youth,
   When Spring weeps her virgin tears;
See that thou rise, too, in the primal truth,
   When the last dread day appears.

Thus they whisper to me in the Autumn day;
   And still when my spirit grieves
I can cheer the gloom and the pain away,
   When I think on the falling leaves.

GRAND OLD THOMAS.

I LIKE my labour and the gods,
   And rave about them in the fashion
Of those who framed their high abodes,
   And fabled them into a passion;
And gave to each the task divine
   Of censor over human action;
With power to quell with nod or sign
   All hot dispute and knotty faction.

I think them yet as bending still
   From their high dwelling-place in kindness,
To give reward for **good** and ill,
   Or punish man **for wilful** blindness.
This is a strange belief, I know,
   And may appear, no doubt, to some **as**
Unworthy of my years ; but **go**
   And lay the blame on "grand old Thomas."

What right had he to come and prate
   About the gods and such digressions,
When I was in that plastic state
   That keeps through lifetime **such** impressions ?
And now, when I have firmer tone,
   And **less unbending in my** nature,
Of gods and faiths **I babble on,**
   And words of German nomenclature.

I also deem this world should leap
   From wonder unto glowing wonder ;
That in its rolling we should keep
   A breast with human feelings under ;
That good should be our aim, and life
   Have more of work and God-like fearing,
And less of all that paltry strife
   That keeps the dirty mud-gods sneering ;

That cant should lift his putrid **wings,**
   And fly back to the primal chaos,
And mix no more in human things,
   Nor with his solemn saws betray us ;
But rot amid the dank abodes,
   Where Styx in silent blackness rushes.
All this came to me when the gods,
   Through "grand **old** Thomas" spoke their **wishes.**

I've less, too, of that iris light
   With **which** " us youth" bedaubs our dreaming ;
And that **which** once was angel bright
   Is back now **to** a human seeming.
I own it cost a pang or two—
   Such price one pays for groping blindly—

But when I felt my clearer view,
    I thank'd the Chelsea Teacher kindly.

I've read your Fènèlon, but he
    Is far too polish'd to my liking;
But " grand old Thomas" speaks to me
    In careless periods, rough and striking.
A Thunder-god is he, whose brow
    Wears its word-lightning to benumb us;
And so *Je crains les dieux* and bow,
    And love and reverence "grand old Thomas."

PAST SPASMODICS.

A LIFE I thought had pass'd away,
    With all its old, spasmodic thinking,
When I read Schiller's " Robber" play,
    Came back upon me swift as winking;
And I was Karl again, and lived
    Through all my dreams and heats in plenty;
From such sweet crimes let me be shrived,
    For I was something short of twenty.

Then grew the world to deeper gloom,
    And took all hues to suit my frenzy,
Even Nature seem'd to find a tomb,
    And droop, as with the influenza;
For I, the mighty Titan still
    (For so I thought myself), was ready
To bend all things to suit my will,
    And keep this *cosmos* rolling steady.

Then I became a robber bold,
    A captain of a band, and dwelt in
A cavern, in whose vortex roll'd
    Those gloomy colours Rembrandt dealt in.
From thence I waged against my kind
    A series of bloodthirsty quarrels,

And at my leisure stored my mind
  With " might was right," and such-like morals.

I had my own Amalia, too,
  Who, when my fellow-kind deserted,
Was still as woman should be—true
  To all my freaks, and tender-hearted ;
And I—her swarthy worshipper—
  Crown'd her with my most daring wishes :
Du liebest mich, I ask'd of her,
  And I received for answer—blushes.

Then came another phase again,
  And I, with deepest wisdom teeming,
Drew my lone self away from men,
  To make them better with my dreaming ;
They came in crowds each day to hear
  My oracles of pith and rigour ;
The Pythia, when her throat was clear,
  Could scarce have match'd their point and vigour.

I tired of this, and next I took
  The hero's sword and freedom's banner,
And wither'd tyrants with my look,
  And slew them in a shocking manner ;
I gave my country liberty,
  And yet—for gratitude is scanty—
If I remember rightly, I
  Was exiled, and I died like Dante.

But wherefore should I lengthen out
  This rhyme with those unhealthy fancies
That came when through the glass of doubt
  I look'd on life with yellow glances?
And such I thought had pass'd away,
  To come no more to set me raving,
Till Schiller, with his nasty play,
  Woke up their old and restless craving.

I never read *Die Räuber* now,
  For fear my early youthful madness

Might come and stamp upon my brow
  Its most prevailing type of sadness;
But *Wilhelm Tell* and *Wallenstein*
  I read, and, reading, feel like magic
The old spasmodic fits decline,
  And dream no more of being tragic.

THE FIRST BREAK.

THE first break in our happy household hearth
  Was my broad manly son, and far away
He sleeps, while by the churchyard's holy earth
  Throb the great engines onward day by day.

Ah me! and as I hear in this strange land
  Their whistle from the distant town, I feel
As if I saw him slipping foot and hand,
  And lying crush'd beneath the heartless wheel.

Then I live o'er again that awful night,
  When to my door the whisper'd message came,
That made my heart leap up with sudden fright,
  And all the silence tremble with his name.

A splash of blood fell everywhere I look'd,
  Turning my tears to the same purple hue,
While in me rose dread fears my heart rebuked,
  As all his vanish'd life rose up to view.

They brought him home, and up the little street
  They bore him slowly to his early rest,
Laying the green sod, that of old his feet
  Had trod in Sabbath days, upon his breast.

He slept, while in my heart I bore the pain
  That still would live at times, until at last
My being's inner depths closed up again,
  And gave but little token of the past.

Then came a change. I left that dear old spot
  Where boyhood, manhood, all had come to me—
Came here among my sons, but never brought
  My **heart,** for that was still beyond the sea.

Yet that one night before I left, I took
  My stand beside his grave, and with hush'd breath,
Raised to the skies a father's silent look,
  And took mute farewell of the dust beneath.

Then, turning as beneath some sudden blight,
  I stagger'd down the churchyard big with fears,
Went down the street for the last time, the night
  Around me hiding all my bitter tears.

I reach'd my lowly home, now cold and dim,
  Sat by the hearth, a shadow **on** my mind,
Thinking how all around me seem'd like him
  Whose dust cost such a pang to leave behind.

I sail'd.   And now between me and that home
  The ocean rolls with never-ceasing moan,
Checking all in me save my dreams, that roam
  To bring old faces nearer to my own.

But still, whenever **from the distant town**
  I hear the engine shriek, **then far away**
I wander to that grave, where up and down,
  Close by his rest, they thunder day **by day.**

THE TWO WATCHWORDS.

First appeared in the *Quiver*, and taken from that **Magazine by kind**
permission of Messrs Cassell, Petter, & Galpin.

Ⅱ HEARD an angel singing in the **air,**
  And looking upward in my fear and dread,
I said, " O thou whose looks and garments are so fair,
  Why sing ye thus so sweetly overhead?"

Then bending in his meekness unto me,
  He answer'd, " I am sent by God to give
Two watchwords unto those who yet may see,
  No bound but that of earth that they may live."

" And who are they," I question'd, " that receive
  This boon of His high grace ?" and he replied,
" The firm in heart, who have the power to sieve
  The restless day, and cast its dregs aside.

" And with the first sweet watchword, which is ' Pray,'
  They move," he said, " in holy fear and trust,
Knowing that He will lead them to his day,
  Which is beyond the realm of death and dust.

" I sing to cheer them that they may not quail,
  Nor shrink amid life's busy toil and pain ;
But if through all the weary fight they fail
  To use the second watchword, all is vain."

And bowing down, methought I heard his wing
  Rustle, to seek the balmy fields above,
When, like the gushing of a second spring,
  Came downward from his lips the watchword—" Love."

OLD ADAM.

OLD Adam breaking stones by the wayside,
  Leans on his hammer for a moment's space,
Then turns away his head, as if to hide
The tears that trickle down his worn and wrinkled face.

I stop with him to hear him talk away,
  But as I see the sorrow in his eye
I question Adam, Why so sad to-day ?
  And, wiping from his check the tears, the old man makes reply—

" Ah, William, I but view'd the past behind,
  And from it rose with clear and open brow

One who was ever warm in heart and **kind,**
  But he **is** in his grave, **and I am lonely** now.

"God knows I loved him **overmuch, and He**
  Seeing some wiser end—to me **unseen—**
Reach'd out His hands from clouds, and **took from** me
  The prop on which **my age had** fondly **hoped** to lean.

" Proud was **I of my boy, and** well **I might,**
  For he, too, **had the gift** of thought **and song ;**
And his I sang **to make my** labour light,
  While he toil'd at his **books,** that mayhap **did him wrong.**

" **I** never sing them **now, save in my** heart,
  Since my **son** died ; **for a drear sound** of **death**
Rolls through their **melody, as if a part**
  Of each, **and** tears come **up and choke my failing** breath.

" **But** aught that **knew** his touch we keep—his books
  From which he drew at night **a** silent bliss,
Though useless now to me with their strange looks,
  I lift them often up because they once were his :

" **And as I sit,** thus in my plodding brain
  I fashion proudly forth what high career
Might have been his, and earnest noble **gain**
  That would have kept me now from toiling feebly here.

" But like the fading **light** within **the west**
  He sank, leaving this earth when he was gone
A sadder sight to me, and **in my** breast
  A grief that seems like **sin, because** it still **lives on.**

" **Then as I** bow, my wife **beside** me stands ;
  ' Adam,' she whispers, **and her** eyes are dim ;
I look, and murmur, as I **clasp** her hands,
  ' Dear wife, our only son, **and** I was set **on him.'**

" But as she speaks, **my grief** begins to sink,
  And all my being grows **warm** with other love,
Born of all hope and faith **that** still will link
  Our highest aims below to **one** great source **above.**

"So as I toil from morn till weary night,
 I teach myself to think that all is wise ;
That what to me is dark shall be made light,
 When I look back on earth with God's own pitying eyes."

THE WHUSSLE.

PLAGUE tak' his auld grannie, wha brocht frae the toon
 That whussle, an' gie'd him't to deave us wi' soun' ;
 For frae mornin' till nicht it's a wheeple an' skirl,
Till my lugs at sic music dae naething but dirl.
But he wheedled her ow'r—'od, he kens, the wee limb,
She wad bring, at his beck, a hale hoosefu' to him—
He's ca'd for her ain man, noo in his lang hame,
Sae nae wunner she tak's to the bairn an' his name.

That nicht when she brocht it, his heart gie'd a loup,
An' though in his first sleep he sat up on his dowp,
Took it into his han', an' he blew wi' sic micht,
That she sat by his bedside an' skreigh'd wi' delicht.
An' aye as he tootled, a prood sleekit smile
Lay on his bit face, her ain safter the while,
An' she half-turn'd her heid as she hearken'd to me—
"Jean, that bairn has the same cheerie twirl o' his e'e."

But since thaun, whaten wark he's had oot in the street,
Tootlin' roun' a' the carts that he happen's to meet,
Or stan'in' for hoors wi' the pigman, big Jock,
As if hired to gie music to draw oot the folk ;
But Jock, kindly body, for daein' the same,
Gie'd him that jug ye see hingin' there wi' his name ;
An' richt prood was he when he cam' hame to tell,
Haudin' 't oot in his glee an airm's length frae himsel'.

But ae Sabbath day, an' my cheek still will burn,
In bounced Mrs Rae, wi' her quick kin' o' turn,
An' she says, "Dae ye ken that your bairn—what a sin!--
Is oot-by wi' his whussle ?—ye should keep him in."

But I thocht for awee, an' says I, " Mrs Rae,
The wean's but a wean, an' ye've naething to say ;
For we a' ken your Tam, wha's sae sleekit an' sly,
Was seen ance at the bools when the kirk folk gaed by."

I was mad at the time, but I gaed my ways oot,
In time just to hear his last flourish an' toot ;
I never loot on, though, but waved wi' my han',
An' cried, " Willie, come in to your dinner, my man."
Sae he cam' slippin' in ; ay, an' wad ye believe ?
The brat had the whussle stuck up his coat-sleeve.
But I sune took it doun, an', for siccan mishap,
Made his hurdies grow closer acqwaunt wi' the strap.

His faither, wha scarce can ken Bonnie Dundee
Frae the solemn Auld Hunner, says aften to me—
" Jean, that bairn 'ill turn oot a musicianer yet,
For ye see weel eneuch that his mooth has the set
For playin' the whussle, the bugle, an' a'
Thae ither twirl'd things that they finger an' blaw ;
Faith ! wha kens but his name 'ill yet spread far and wide,
While we'll no can conceal frae the neebors oor pride ?"

I aye shake my heid, though I think sae mysel',
For though steerin' he's gleg i' th' uptak' an' fell ;
An' for music—d'ye ken that he even maun keep
His whussle in min', an' blaw on't in his sleep ?
An' whiles when I wauken an' catch him at this,
'Od, I cuddle him closer, an' gie him a kiss ;
While my heart swalls within me, an' grows unco fain,
To think that I hae sic a musical wean.

They may talk o' their great Paganini, an' sing
About what he could dae just on ae fiddle string,
But for me, when I see my ain bairnie oot-by
Gaun sidy for sidy wi' ane just as sly,
Keeping time on an auld roosted tray to his toots,
Like twa Lilliput sergeants sent oot for recruits,
Losh, I fin' that his wheeples are dearer to me
Than a' their fine twirls that they fetch ow'r the sea.

THE DEAD MOTHER.

THE feeble infant, but an hour in life,
   Lay wailing in our arms, while on the bed
Slept, like a faded flower, the one year's wife,
   With all her mother's first sweet feelings, dead.

She slept ; and on her lips, all shrunk and white,
   A smile lay faint, as when a sunbeam lies
Upon a wither'd leaf, then pass'd away
   In the dark sorrow of her drooping eyes.

Her hands were folded in a quiet rest
   Upon her bosom fair, and round, and smooth,
As if in death she held to that fair breast
   The first fond pledge of wedded love and youth.

Ah me ! what wealth of love and soft appeal,
   With all the holiest of human bands,
Lay silent in that breast, no more to feel
   The soothing touch of little lips and hands.

Even as we gazed, upon her cold, still face,
   Grew forth a yearning wish some boon to grant,
As if her spirit had heard from its high place
   Lips moaning still for all their earliest want.

Each look'd at each, as one who understands ;
   We rose with tortured thoughts in our despair,
And from her breast unwound her claspéd hands,
   And laid the infant for a moment there.

It might be fancy, but we thought her face
   Grew bright, and that her pitying eyelids shone
With large, glad tears that left a dewy trace ;
   But these might fall in sorrow from our own.

Then kneeling, in our hearts like some sweet psalm
   Rose up the past with all its tender seal,

While the near future came and laid its balm
    Upon that life those dead arms could not feel—

That little one which through **our tears we saw**
    Moving its tiny fingers all around,
While lips that could not use their gentle law
    Moan'd—and no mother's voice to soothe their sound.

Dust unto dust ; we rose and softly took
    The helpless one away, and with **hush'd** breath
Reclasp'd her hands, then bent for one last look,
    Kiss'd **the cold** lips, **and** left the rest **to** death.

O human hearts, this world **is God's, and we**
    Who walk within the glory **of** His smile
Grow blind at times with such great light, **nor see**
    How all works unto fruitful ends the while ;

This world is God's, and in each heart-eclipse
    Shadows **but** rise that faith and hope may **view**
Through the tear-rainbow'd gloom, with praising lips,
    His finger from the heavens pointing through.

THE BOWL O' SENNA LEAF.

A' the ills that come to swall a wearit mither's grief,
    The warst is when her laddie winna tak' his senna leaf ;
    An' here I've stood this ae half-hour, the berries in the spune,
An' yet he winna drink it up to get them when it's dune.

Plague **tak' his faither, wha boo'd** say sae thochtfu' unto me—
" Get **oot the ither** teapot, Bell, an' gie the wean some tea."
The rogue heard **(for he's gleg's a** hawk), an' noo he tak's his han's,
An' pushes back **the bowl, an'** shiles, an' kicks the table ban's.

I dinna ken what plan to **tak' to** mak' him swallow this,
For **if** I tell him that he'll **dee,** he kensna what it is,
An' big Daft Jock, wha slings aboot an' fears the village weans,
Has nae **poo'r ow'r** this rogue o' mine, wha lauchs at a' my pains.

Weel, weel, my man ; **your** faither comes to tak' his sowp at twae,
An' if I tell him a' the truth, what think ye will he say ?
He winna lick his bairn, I ken—he maistly tak's his pairt—
But he'll tell the joiner no **to** heed to mak' his braw new cairt.

Losh, hae I hit the nail at last ? He turns aboot his heid,
An' raxes oot his han' in haste to dae the awfu' deed ;
Three mouthfu's tak's the senna oot, anither cleans the spoon,
Twa thraws or three o' his bit mou', an' that sair task is dune.

I canna think but Clootie stan's the very same as me,
An' coaxes bigger weans **to** come and taste his hell-brewn tea ;
Wha, when they tak' a sowp, an' fin' he has them in his poo'r,
They own the tea was unco sweet, the berries awfu' soor.

BLIND MATTHEW.

First appeared in the *Quiver*, and taken from that Magazine by kind
permission of Messrs Cassell, Petter, & Galpin.

BLIND Matthew, coming down **the** village street
    With slow, **sure** footsteps, pauses for a while,
And in **the** sunlight falling soft and sweet
    His features brighten to a kindly smile.

Upon his ear the sounds of toil and gain,
    Clanking from wood-girt shop and smithy, **steal,**
And soft he whispers, " O my fellow-men,
    I cannot see you, but I hear and feel."

Then smiling still he slowly steps along,
    And every kindly word and friendly tone,
Like the old fragment of an early song,
    Wakes thoughts that make the past again his own.

The children see him, and in merry band
    Come shouting from their glad and healthy **play,**
" Here is blind Matthew, let us take his hand,
    And **see if** he can guess our names to-day."

Then all around him throng, and run, and press,
  And lead him to his seat beneath the tree,
Each striving to be first, for his caress,
  Or gain the favour'd seat upon his knee.

Then Matthew, happy in their artless prate,
  Cries, as he slips into their guileless plan,
" Now she who holds my right hand is sweet Kate,
  And she who holds my left is little Anne."

Then all the children leap with joyful cries,
  Till one fair prattler nestling on his breast
Whispers, " Blind Matthew, tell us when thine eyes
  Shall have their light, and open like the rest."

Then closer still he draws the little one,
  Laying his hand upon her golden head ;
Then speaks with low, soft, sweet and solemn tone,
  While all the rest range round with quiet tread.

He tells how Christ, in ages long ago,
  Came down to earth in human shape and name,
Walking his pilgrimage, begirt with woe,
  And laying healing hands on blind and lame.

Then of blind Bartimeus, the beggar, he
  Who by the wayside sat, and cried in awe,
" Jesus, thou Son of David, look on me ;"
  And Jesus look'd and touch'd him, and he saw.

" But not on earth these orbs of mine shall fill
  With light," thus Matthew ends, " for in this night
I must grope on with Christ to guide me still,
  And He will lead me through the grave to light.

" So when you miss old Matthew from the street,
  And in the quiet of the churchyard lies
A new-made grave, to draw your timid feet,
  Then will you know that Christ has touch'd my eyes."

RACHEL.

RACHEL, soft and shy and blushing, pass'd into the angel wife,
  Tears of joy within the rapture of her sweetly-drooping eyes;
  While an Iris, many-colour'd, overarch'd her novel life,
  Like the first sweet gush of sunlight sloping down on Paradise.

Then, with head bent in her meekness, slowly did she turn away;
  Heard a rough yet manly voice make music in her raptured ear;
Leant upon an arm that through this life was now her wish'd-for
      stay;
  Heart! but in such time the heavens surely must be very near.

So she pass'd into her home, and stood upon the shining hearth,
  Heaven's mission, like a halo, resting on her queenly head;
And her lips and eyes had parted with their dear old maiden's
      mirth
  For a staider look and gladness that were springing up instead.

Happy now with him, her idol, like the cadence of a song,
  Swept the days above her, adding sweetness to her tender dream,
Till at last, as comes the tempest, burst upon her head a wrong,
  Blighting all her life, as trees that shrink before the lightning's
      gleam.

Standing by the doorway looking in the evening light for him,
  Lo! a band of rugged faces with a solemn burden come,
And they bear it o'er the threshold, mangled in the face and limb;
  "Killed at his work," they whisper, and they stand beside her,
      dumb!

O, the wail of woman's sorrow, heard in Heaven's highest place!
  Sister angels bowing lowly, as if weeping holy tears,
Till they look again and catch upon the heavenly Father's face
  All the wisdom that we see not for our paltry human fears.

Rachel knelt beside him, laid his head upon her throbbing breast—
  Ah! beneath it beat a little life that soon would see the light;
Kiss'd his lips and eyes that knew not why they were so madly
      press'd;
  Called his name, but all was silent as the slowly coming night.

Silent round the dead and living, as beneath some potent spell,
   Stood the rough forms, tann'd with labour, looking down on
      human grief,
Till within their own deep hearts the tears began to throb and
   swell,
   And rise slowly upward, giving to their pent-up breath relief.

Then they took her from the dead, that soon must rest within the
      grave,
   Weak and weary as an infant with the tears that she had wept ;
But when she woke again to feel her loss and moan and rave,
   Her life's broken idol calmly in the village churchyard slept.

Then the kindly ones that watch'd through weary nights her bitter
      pain
   Whisper'd softly to each other, " All this grief will never cease
Till the baby comes, and with it Heaven's healing light again,
   That shall crown her mother's being with its perfect rest and
      peace."

And it came—a tiny thing, its father's cherish'd name to bear—
   Lay within her arms the harbinger of God's wide love below ;
And her life broke from its grief, and took to channels clear and fair,
   Something of her old life's music mingling in its quiet flow.

So when night came down on Rachel, with its deep celestial calm,
   And the past rose upward—sacred in her eyes for evermore—
And her baby in her bosom slumber'd, breathing hope's own balm,
   Then her heart fill'd up with blessings at the joy she had in store.

Ye who in this world's darkness stand, and see no star to guide—
   God's left hand from out the shadows laid upon your head to
      smite—
Bow, and in your heart despair not, flinging restless doubts aside,
   For ye know not all the good He holds within His right.

AGNES.

*First appeared in Chambers' Journal, and taken from that Journal by
kind permission of W. & R. Chambers.*

OPEN again the garden door,
　When the flowers live their little time,
And I stand as you used to stand before
　By the rose-bush in its prime.

And I pluck one bud from the loaden'd stem,
　This is for you I say ;
Then I take a leaf from the glowing gem,
　And fling the rest away.

Now why should I place this single leaf
　Where my other treasures lie,
And why should I keep it like the grief
　That is seen in a thoughtful eye ?

I keep it because it was thus you stood,
　That golden afternoon,
Plucking a rose in your maiden mood,
　And humming a low, sweet tune.

Humming a low, sweet tune alone,
　And watching with half a smile
The fairy rose-leaves that were strewn
　Around your feet the while.

And I stood in the shade of the garden door,
　And heard you at your song,
And saw the rich leaves downward pour
　As the low winds came along.

Now, when death has pluck'd your life's sweet bud,
　And your footsteps are heard no more,
I think it a joy to stand where you stood,
　By the rose at the garden door.

So I creep in as beneath some fear
  And pluck with trembling hand
A rose from the bush you held so dear
  Ere you went to the spirit land.

And I take one leaf from the bud—no more—
  Then fling the rest away,
And turn again to the garden door
  In the golden summer day.

And I whisper, " The bud that I resign
  Is thy clay to its own earth given ;
But the leaf that I keep is that spirit of thine
  With its incense—all of heaven."

ANNA.

I LOVED her when I was at school—
  So early Cupid flung his fetter ;
I fought my rivals, like a fool,
  And thrash'd them, for I knew no better,
Of course I was not very strong,
  And I could count my years eleven ;
But then my head was free from song,
  And careless of the Muse's heaven.

She ruled me with a queen-like power—
  She sat supreme o'er all my fancies ;
I flung to her at every hour,
  Broadcast, a thousand tender glances ;
And when at times we two would stand
  Together, busy lessons plying,
I used to touch her gentle hand,
  And feel it give a mute replying,

But then the happiest time for me
  Was when the patron saint of lovers
Came smiling round, and I was free
  To place my vows in fancy covers ;

I sent her many a work of art,
   Whose each design was Cupid ranging
To fix an arrow in a heart,
   With this for motto—" All unchanging."

She sent me one—I keep it still—
   Two hands bound with a rosy tether,
Below a church upon a hill, .
   To which went couples link'd together.
Ah, me! what many a dream and vow
   Rose up with such before my vision!
I prized it then as you would now
   A Raphael, Rembrandt, or a Titian.

Well, things went on, as things will roam,
   And, in the course of our sweethearting,
I used to see her half-way home,
   And take a little kiss at parting;
And still as Cupid plied his strife,
   And all my passion growing bolder,
She promised she would be my wife,
   But I must be a little older.

O heaven! years have flown away,
   And leaves have turn'd from green to yellow
Since then, and I have had to-day
   A letter from an old schoolfellow,
Who tells me she I loved of yore—
   Then sweet as some Aurora Raby—
Is married now a year and more,
   And I'm to come and see her baby.

Now what have I do but call
   The muse that mourns o'er vanish'd glory,
And write another Locksley Hall,
   And be the hero of the story?
Or—but as earthly things below
   Are made to fade, however pleasant,
I'll smile the past away, and go
   And give the little imp a present.

A PARTING.

First appeared in *Cassell's Magazine*, and taken from that Magazine by kind permission of Messrs Cassell, Petter, and Galpin.

THE sunlight fell through the shadowy trees
  In smiles all soft and sweet,
While the incense breath of an early breeze
  Stirr'd the primrose at our feet.

And you stoop'd to pluck its round bright eye
  That peep'd up to the day,
Then turn'd from its golden bloom with a sigh,
  For your thoughts were far away.

Ay, far away with some dearer one,
  And hearing within your ear,
Breath'd out in love's low undertone,
  The vows that you loved to hear.

I knew I had no share in your heart,
  And yet I could but speak,
While my life's sweet thoughts began to start
  With the blush upon your cheek.

But you whisper'd as light as a leaf when turn'd
  By the breath of the wooing wind,
A low sweet whisper, as if it mourn'd
  For the pain it left behind.

And your eyes for a moment met my own
  With the love that might have been,
Then slowly sank, and their light was gone,
  And the sunlight fell between.

Ah me! through that sunlight I see thee now,
  With the old-love-bloom on your cheek,
And within your eyes the same sweet glow
  Of the thoughts you would not speak.

H

Then my heart, like a pilgrim, makes its choice,
    And flings all thoughts away,
And listens again to thy low sweet voice,
    As thine own did to *his* that day.

FIRST LOVE.

I LOOK back to my early life,
    When I was seventeen or so ;
When Love first shed his rosy strife,
    And made my brain and bosom glow.
When first a maiden, full of grace,
    And fair as the wild flowers of Spring,
Came smiling from some fairy place,
    And made my life a golden thing.

I worshipp'd her as all divine—
    I worshipp'd her with glorious truth ;
I flung upon that early shrine
    The brightest hopes that fed my youth.
I wrote in many a secret rhyme,
    Her charms of brow and neck of snow ;
I held such poems then sublime—
    I burn'd them three long years ago.

I built up many a lordly dome—
    Alladin's could not cope with mine ;
In Fancy's car I brought her home,
    And whisper'd to her, " All is thine."
I knelt before her, free from doubt,
    To kiss the hand that wore the ring ;
I woke up. Jove ! The fire was out,
    And found that there was no such thing.

To sing of all my fits and whims,
    And raptures of that golden time,
The bliss fit match for a cherubim's
    Were all beyond my powers of rhyme.

Suffice it, when the bubble burst,
  And I was left to weep and blame,
I thought of doing some deed accursed
  As worthy of my blighted name.

I sang, in real Byronic strain,
  My woes to every listening tree ;
The wind sang chorus to my pain,
  And howl'd in sympathy with me.
I wrote my epitaph each day,
  To grace **my** lone, romantic rest.
I'm living **still,** and, strange to say,
  There's no romance about **my breast.**

But is that maiden **now** forgot,
  And all the warmth **of long ago ?**
Ah, no ! She lives still in my thought,
  But not with such an angel glow.
For years have come, and I the while
  See human things are less divine ;
But still, if you would have me smile,
  Don't mention that first love of mine.

THOSE FOOTSTEPS.

First appeared in *Cassell's Magazine,* and taken from that Magazine by kind permission of Messrs Cassell, Petter, & Galpin.

IN the quiet hush **of the tender night,**
  When my eyes fill up with tears,
Comes my darling **unto** me, all golden bright
  With the sunshine of three sweet years.

And he smiles as he climbs to his seat on my knee,
  To whisper his childish mirth ;
Then clasps my neck—though you may not see,
  For my darling is not of earth.

Not of this cold damp earth of ours,
  That betimes, in its freaks **of love,**

Plucks away the buds from our sweetest flow'rs
    To open them up above.

So I knew that my darling, though not with me,
    Is in heaven an angel bright;
And the form that climbs up to his seat on my knee
    Is the shadow of him to-night.

But this shadow meets me now no more
    Half-a-mile from my lowly home,
Nor is seen in the shade of the half-shut door,
    Awaiting until I come.

Only within the twilight gloom,
    When the hours are long and sweet,
I hear all about in the lonely room
    The patter of little feet—

Patter of feet that come and go
    With a sweet yet restless will,
Just as they did a month ago,
    Ere they grew for ever still.

And my heart, at those spirit-sounds that seem
    So near yet so far away,
Glides into the faith of a sweet love-dream,
    That follows me night and day.

And this love-dream, tender and ever sweet,
    Still whispers soft and low—
" Keep thou in thy heart these tiny feet,
    And follow the way they go."

Then my sorrow sinks down as a leaflet will
    When the winds are into their rest ;
And I bow with claspèd hands, and still
    The footsteps are in my breast.

WEE TOTTIE.

WEE TOTTIE'S the smile that lichts up oor hearthstane—
A dumpy bit thing that can scarce gang her lane ;
Yet what aul'-farrant gab comes at times frae her mou',
As she sits on oor knee, wi' her hair ow'r her broo.

For she tells what she'll dae wi' her wee han's abreed,
An' what she'll no dae wi' a shake o' her heid ;
Then lilts some bit sang, wi' her ain kin' o' glee,
Though nae singer, atweel, is her faither or me.

An' she gies siccan names, that we ne'er heard afore,
To the tables, the chairs, to the cupboard, an' door ;
Then lauchs, wi' a lauch sweet an' clear as a bell,
At her ain Hebrew lore, that nane kens but hersel'.

Then she thrummels the leaves o' some aul' tatter'd book,
Readin' into hersel' wi' a mak'-believe look ;
Then, seein' nae pictures to please her e'e there,
Tears a leaf oot for papers to curl up her hair.

But, O, if ye saw her, sae wife-like and droll,
When she gets her bit plaidie to carry her doll,
Hoo she whisks roun' the en's o't, then dumps through the hoose,
Like a Lilliput mither tosh, sonsie and douce.

Then, after she gies her wee baby a sook,
She rows't up sae cozy and lays't in some nook ;
Then, wearied hersel', creeps up on to my knee,
Rubs her een, an' my dawtie's as soun' as can be.

So wee Tottie maun gang to her bed an' sleep soun',
While fairies through a' the still nicht hover roun'—
Sleep, sleep till the mornin', then rise a' her lane,
An' be her ain mither's Wee Tottie again.

THE CHILD'S GRAVE.

IT was a little grave—
So little, you could almost think the sexton
Had, in his weary labour, left a sod—
A single sod, upon the churchyard grass,
Intending to remove it when he saw
The mould appearing through a larger grave.

And yet it was a grave whose tiny chasm
Held the dear ashes of a little one
Whose life was far too good, and fair, and beautiful
For this black world of ours to touch and soil.

And so it pass'd away, as will a flower
That feels the frost of Autumn.   Day by day
The cheek grew bright and brighter as the soul
Wearied for freedom ; and to bend and look
Upon the features one could almost think
That Heaven itself could make no change, but set
A golden crown upon the little head,
And flowing raiment on the little form,
To fit it for some pitying angel's breast.
So all was finish'd, and it went away ;
And there were bitter tears around the bed,
And many wishes, such as ever spring
From the rich soil within the tender breast
Of her who is a mother, and whose grief
Is so within itself that none can know
Its depth or feeling : it is much akin
To theirs whose soul is on the very edge
Of an eternity, and who, to give
Comfort to those around, will utter words
Of faith, and hope, and love, and happier meetings
Within another land, where there shall be
No more disunions, and have but to turn
An eye within, and find a hopeless gloom.

So was the mother's grief.   But she had Hope,
Who whisper'd to her of a better time,

When she, for surety, would receive again
The firstling of her womb from Him whose kingdom
Is made of such, and, in a brighter bloom
Than in its gladdest days upon the earth
When life was in its flush, and Death had set
No mark upon the little brow, to show
The sepulchre its consecrated own.

O, dear, dear ashes that are nought but dross
To the sweet spirit that in realms above
Blooms in all purity, and yet our hearts
Must linger, like a miser at his gold,
Around the little sod that hides the form
That heaven gave to us for such a short
And fleeting period.

Now years have come
And flung a calm upon this grief of ours,
And we can look within the past, and find
That all was fraught with wisdom, and can bend
A knee to the Almighty, with a heart
Purer and freer from unholy wishes
Than when we laid it, with a bitter heart,
Within the chambers of an early grave.

HE CAME FROM A LAND.

HE came from a land whose shadows
    Were brighter than our day ;
And he sang of the streams and meadows,
    And then he went away.

Now I turn from the heart that ever
    Will moan for the clay behind ;
When the soul is such glorious liver
    In the boundless realms of mind.

So at night when the shadows grow dreary,
    And a sorrow is in my breast,

And the wings of life grow weary,
   And flutter as if for rest :

Then I open my little book-case,
   When the quiet is breathing low,
And I take from the shelf in silence
   A volume of long ago.

And I read and read by the firelight
   Till quick and clear as chimes
The man himself is with me,
   And is talking to me in rhymes.

Talking of waving meadows
   And cunningly-hidden brooks,
With the quietest gush of eddies
   That the flowers may see their looks.

Babbling of summer and sunshine,
   And hills that reach the cloud ;
And this—all this in whispers,
   For he never speaks aloud.

Then betimes when I shut the volume
   To walk in the quiet street,
When the stars, which are shadows of angels,
   Have made the silence sweet :

He follows me still like a presence
   That none but spirits see ;
And at every pause of my footstep
   His music is speaking to me.

Whispers and speaks till the night-time
   So trembles with all its tone
That I cannot but let my being
   Move into the clasp of his own.

So whenever I lift the volume,
   Like summer-beams that glow,
That spirit comes out from the silence
   And babbles of long ago.

O O R   S I S.

OR Sis is a mitherly sort o' a bairn,
An unco gleg thing, an' sae easy to learn,
That let her see ance hoo a thing should be dune,
An' ye've nae trouble wi' her or fash afterhin' ;
An' she does a' wi' siccan a look on her broo—
Sae thochtfu' an' womanlike aye to oor view—
That we wunner an' try tae fin' oot, but in vain,
Hoo sic auld-fashion'd thochts got a haud o' oor wean.

Then she speirs sic wise questions that frae her seem droll,
As she cuts oot some shapin's for goons to her doll,
An' a' aboot weans that she wants us to tell,
As if she was some wrinkled granny hersel',   .
That I look on her whiles wi' a sort o' a fear,
As if something unseen or uncanny was near,
Tittlin' to her in whispers, as laigh as can be,
A' thae queer thochts o' hers that in turn puzzle me.

She's the first that fin's oot a' the holes in the breeks
O' her brithers, dear rogues, wha are sair on their steeks ;
Then she'll thraw her bit mou', an' she'll peenge, an' she'll wheedle,
Till I get oot my thummle, a pirn, an' a needle ;
An' the rascals, to keep things in cosie hame rule,
Maun e'en lay themsel's ow'r her wee creepie stool,
While I guide her wee han' wi' the thread through an' through,
An' losh, but it's leesome hoo weel she can shoo.

Then, when washin' day comes for oor ain dirty duds,
What a wark she has after't amang the saip suds !
But first I maun row up her wee frock ahin',
An' get some auld cloot an' draw't through 'neath her chin ;
Then she scoors her bit duds, wrings them oot in a fyke,
An' spreads them to dry on the en' o' the dyke,
Rinnin' oot noo an' then as if fley'd for the rain—
What a wife she will mak' to somebody, oor wean !

An' just but last night I made saps to wee Jean—
She's oor youngest, new spean'd, an' she's waukrife at e'en—

What does Sis dae but gang an' mak' some o' her ain,
An' fleech wi' her big billy, Jock, to be wean:
An' Jock—he's no miss'd for a stammuck—sat doon,
His han's at his back, an' mooth wide for the spoon,
An' she fed him fu' weel, as he sat on his doup,
Scrapin' mooth, cheek, an' chin atween every sowp.

She has just ae wee faut, but it's ane we can thole—
She wad 'maist gie ye ocht for an auld parasol;
An' l min' when oor neebor next door gi'ed her ane
She had faun' in the press, a' moth-eaten an' dune,
She was sae ta'en up wi't that, let what weather fa',
She aye took it oot as a biel' frae them a',
Till at last, for fair shame's sake, I burn'd it, an sair
Did she greet when she kenn'd she wad get it nae mair.

But she's siccan a helpfu' bit thing, an' sae kin',
That what fau'ts she has canna stop lang on the min';
But whether she rocks wi' a prim, modest face,
The cradle, or looks in her wee tittie's face,
Or washes the laigh single step at oor door,
Or looks oot for dad when his day's wark is o'er,
Or toddles aboot on some wark o' her ain,
She's aye oor wee Sis—my ain mitherly wean.

A SPIRIT IS SINGING A SONG.

A SPIRIT is singing a song somewhere,
    As I go out to my work—
Singing aloud in the open air
    And wherever echoes lurk.

Now I say to myself, " What spirit is this
    That pipes so clear and strong;
For it cannot be a bird, I wis,
    That sings such a wondrous song.

Yet, if bird it be that with such an art
   Pours out this melody,
Then a mighty spirit is in his heart
   When he sings this song to me.

But I take the other side, and say—
   Of spirits there is a dearth ;
And angels but seldom come this way
   To pipe a song on earth.

And poets cannot live in the air
   As doth that one white cloud,
Or I would say that one was there,
   And was thinking his thoughts aloud."

But, whether he poet be or bird,
   He pipes full well and strong,
And hath the gift that can make him be heard
   Whatever may be his song.

For such gushes of mellow music come
   Upon the drinking ear,
That what song I claim as mine is dumb
   When a singer like this is near.

Hark ! how the balmy notes are raised
   But to fall in a golden gush ;
O, fool, whom a poet's lore has crazed,
   Have you never heard the thrush ?

JOCK BUCHAN.

I STILL min' Jock Buchan, the lang gawkie fule,
  He was nearly man muckle though still at the schule,
While I was a laddie the penny book in,
Just trying for knowledge, though sweer to begin.

I see him the noo, lang, ungainly, uncouth,
Wi' red flabby cheeks an' a slaverin' mooth,

Runnin' through the schule green wi' a hap, step, and jump,
His bare waukit heels on the stanes playin' dump.

He was sent to the schule by his weel-meanin' fowk,
Wha thocht that their puir silly innocent gowk
Wad be far better there, gettin' sense in his croon,
Than rinnin' stravaigin' through a' the hale toon.

He read in the Testament a' by himsel',
An O what a treat when he started to spell;
For he whurr'd, an' the " r's" in his throat wad dispute,
As if fechtin' for wha wad be first to get oot.

When he started to spell he wad gie a bit hoast,
Then the laighmost clear button his waiskit could boast
He wad grup, an' unbutton, an' button, an' spell,
Makin' words o' six letters as lang as himsel'.

I hae often inspeckit wi' roun' glow'rin' e'en,
That aul' button-hole where nae thread could be seen;
Tryin', bairn-like, to fin' oot, but aye a' in vain,
Some link atween it an' his ain silly brain.

When the schule scail'd at nicht Jock was aye the first oot,
For this was a hobby he carried aboot;
But, in justice to him an' his hobby, we ken
That mony a dafter's amang wiser men.

When the simmer time cam', bringin' bools o' a' hues—
The piggies, the sprecklies, the blue waterloos—
Tam's fancy was aye for a piggie weel burn'd
(He aye ca'd them glaizies), a' ithers he spurn'd.

He wad question me aft, in his ain thowless way,
"Sand-y hif ye ony gul-azies the day?"
An' if I had ane that attrackit his e'e,
He wad make for a barter, an' offer me three.

Three aul' common piggies, o' dull, dirty white,
Nae wunner he wanted them oot o' his sight;
A' was gowd that to him had a glitter, an' fain,
At that time, I maun own, his belief was my ain.

There was ae thing 'bout **Jock I ne'er** could understan' ;
He wad come to me whiles, **haudin'** oot his lang han',
Then kick up his **heels wi' a** flourish, an' **say,**
" Ah, ye didna, **ye miss'd it,"** an' **then rin away.**

What his 'en **was for this was a riddle to me,**
An' will be, **I doubt, till the day that I dee ;**
But if ony **aul' schulemate could solve** me the **same,**
I wad sen' **him an** autograph **letter to frame.**

When **Jock** ran an erran', wi' some easy task,
He wad knock at **the door, an'** then solemnly ask—
" Mistress, d'ye **keep ony cats** in the hoose ?"
If the answer **was " No,"** he wad enter **fu' croose.**

To explain this odd question : **When he was a wean**
He chackit his big tae wi' **some** muckle **stane,**
An', sittin' ae nicht at **the fire** wi't a' bare,
Save a slice o' fat bacon for healin' the sair,

The cat, that was purrin' upon the cheekstane,
Thocht into hersel' that a feast was her ain,
Made **a spring,** took the bacon, **but left** the **big tae,**
An' **alang wi't a hate for** her kin' **to this day.**

I hae seen **Jock but ance since I** left that aul' schule,
An' he still **was the same fozie,** lang-leggit fule,
That I, half-forgettin', stood waitin' to hear
A deman' for gul-azies, or ithers as **queer.**

When I raise to come **oot, for the sake o'** langsyne,
I gie'd him **some** bawbees **to keep me in min' ;**
He drawl'd **oot** his thanks **wi' his aul'** usual spell,
Push'd me back from the chair, an' sat doon in't himsel'.

Weel, **to come to an** end, as **I** scribbled this rhyme,
Came a langin' **to see** him just ae ither time ;
So I think, ere **the trees** tak' their vesture o' broon,
I maun gang **an' see Jock in his ain native toon.**

NIGHT IN THE VILLAGE.

THE street to-night is empty,
  And the last slow footstep gone ;
The windows grow darker and darker,
  And I am left alone.

And I stand and hear the whisper
  Of the breeze that along the street
Comes, pausing by each dim doorway
  Like some magician's feet ;

While far away, from the river,
  Comes a low dread sound that seems
Like the warning we hear at midnight
  When the dead take a part in our dreams.

So in the hush of this night-time,
  When the better thoughts arise,
I turn from the past to the future
  With a softer light in my eyes.

For I feel no more within me
  The old dead thoughts that came
In the earlier years, and pointed
  To the wreath and the poet's name.

But I think of the dead who slumber,
  From the care and the sorrow free ,
And I whisper as soft as the night wind—
  "They are better far than me."

For they teach me this life is nothing
  But a bubble from the first,
Blown out by some cunning spirit
  For the hand of death to burst.

Then what do we toil and strive for
  In this world, still torn and vex'd,
But to show that our faiths are selfish,
  And have no belief in the next?

I look, and the stars above me
  Beam on in their strength and truth,
And smile and watch over the village
  With looks of eternal youth.

I watch in the great wide heaven
  Their changing lustre play,
Till the old soul sinks in my bosom,
  Like night at approach of day.

But I doubt again, and I whisper,
  " O stars, that above me shine,
Will the thoughts that are with me this night-time
  Ever follow this life of mine ?"

Then they wane, and they dance, and they flicker,
  And by this at once I know
That this life is a flux and reflux,
  Till the dust is laid below.

So I turn from the street with a sadness
  Creeping upward within the breast,
To think that the better purpose
  Is so fickle to the test ;

And that the calm of this night time,
  Soothing all like a summer rain,
Is but as a lull in the tempest
  Which to-morrow will wake again.

THE OLD RUINS.

AH, the stream by the ruin in the wood
  Has long ago run dry,
And the only voice in the solitude
  Is the wind that rushes by.

And human work has shared its fate,
　　And the ruins are old and green,
And you push aside the rotten gate,
　　But no living form is seen.

And you step where weeds spring into birth,
　　Where flowers grew up of yore,
But you look in vain for human mirth
　　Through the nettles at the door.

Yet I like to come in the sober eve
　　And stand in this decay,
And build from out the things that grieve
　　A gladness pass'd away.

Then I see in those quaint dreamings still
　　A cottage neat and fair,
With a window looking to the hill,
　　And a rose tree climbing there.

And I see in the doorway a maiden meek,
　　In her novel duty rife,
With the blushes yet upon her cheek
　,　At the gentle name of wife.

Then I hear, as the night comes stealing on,
　　The prattle of little words,
And a manly voice that takes up the tone,
　　And echoes in deeper chords.

Then I see before the half-shut door,
　　In the wavy heat of day,
Just by the stream that leaps no more,
　　A band of children play.

And I hear the light sweet laugh that springs
　　From the prison of the breast,
Like a bird that leaps with joyous wings
　　Above her hidden nest.

Then I see tall youths and maidens fair
　　Around the evening hearth,

And a grey-hair'd sire and a mother there,
Who smile on their happy mirth.

But a shadow creeps down on the light I see,
And withers as with a blight
The once-sweet picture, that never can be
Brought out from the past's still night.

Then I waken up from my dreams at this,
As if a voice had said,
" Now what is the sum of human bliss
When that which had life is dead ?"

So I turn away from the ruins again,
Half-wroth that I should dream,
But stop where the footbridge steps in vain
Across the vanish'd stream.

I look for a moment over the ledge
To see the grasses spring,
And trail their length within the edge,
Where the stream was wont to sing.

But a sadder question within me starts,
As I turn from all I view ;
For where, O where, are human hearts,
When they dry their channels too ?

GRETCHEN.

I SIT by the narrow window,
Ere the summer sunlight dies,
And before me the " Faust" of Goethe,
In its strange, sweet rhythm lies.

And I read till the poet's music
Flashes back to that vanish'd time

I

When my life had the same wild longing
⸱ That frets through his mystic rhyme.

And my heart was full of the yearning
    For some wide good to be ;
But the rougher being of manhood
    Hath still'd that frenzy in me.

But still when I read of Gretchen,
    So simple, and pure, and fair,
And her dear love-dream in the garden,
    Ere the heart felt the deeper snare :

Then I turn to the past, and a maiden
    That came in her gentle might,
And my life at her touch, like the Memnon,
    Gave answers of love and delight.

And again I walk in the moonlight,
    And again look into her eyes,
And see in their depths, like magic,
    The veil of my being rise.

And far in its sunny distance,
    Hope rising upon each hope,
As the full-breasted clouds in summer
    Shoot up through the azure scope.

But those hopes have faded and darken'd,
    From the light that used to be ;
And are now like the evening twilight
    That is creeping in upon me.

But still, when some master poet,
    Who hath felt the same sweet strife,
Stirs up with his full, deep music
    The ashes of that old life :

Then I turn to one sweet vision
    That is set in the years behind,
As the first bright glimpse of a picture
    May lie in a painter's mind :

And again I dream of the maiden—
  The whisper and clasp of love,
Her hand in my own, and the moonlight
  Falling downward from above.

ON THE ENGINE AGAIN.

ONCE more on the mighty engine, boys,
  With my hand on the driver's arm,
And again at his touch through each fire-leading vein
  Throbs a flood of the life-giving charm.
Then away he speeds as a light in the north
  Shooting up makes the heavens grow pale ;
At my feet the glow and the beat of his heart,
  And beneath them the ring of the rail.

Hurrah ! how each sweep of his lightning limb
  Flashes swifter than that of the last,
While, wild as the flight in the dream of the night,
  The distance is galloping past.
On, on, with a madder desire in his breast
  For the space that is yet to be run,
Till a dozen of wires stretching out on my right
  Seem to narrow and rush into one.

How my blood flushes up, like wine dash'd in a cup,
  At the headlong speed of his race,
While he shrieks in his glee, and looks back at me,
  And flings his breath in my face.
Half a world is left in the distance behind,
  Yet he never slacks in his stride,
Nor a drop of sweat is seen glancing yet
  On the iron girths of his side.

Hurrah ! I lean over and pat his neck,
  As a rider might that of his horse,
While beat goes my heart like a Cyclops at work,
  At this terrible acme of force.

I hear the ring of the rail, and the click
   Of the joint, as he roars o'er his track,
And I shriek in my frenzy."A steed for the gods
   Or some Titan Mazeppa to back."

By heaven ! but this would have been the one
   To have hurl'd with a snort and shriek
From the door of his temple, the battle car
   Of the warrior god of the Greek ;
Or have led the front of those coursers that spin,
   Say half-a-dozen abreast,
And whirl the sun, through a dust of clouds,
   To his purple home in the west.

And I think that he fathoms my thoughts, for his form
   Seems to wilder energy strung,
And gleams as might that of the Laöcoon
   When the last dread circle was flung ;
Or it may be, in wrath when he looks behind
   To leap at the light-shapen elf,
And hurl him beneath the wild rush of his feet,
   And take the reins to himself.

I turn, and lo ! with a flash and glare
   His breast is thrown open to see,
And I start in affright at the wild, fierce light
   That is leaping to clutch at me.
Then I whisper, the bloodless fear on my lip,
   As the flame tongues flicker and dance—
"God, he too has a fire round his heart, like those kings
   In the Eblis hall of romance !"

But this fire within him is the nerve in his limb,
   And his pulse's hurry and shock,
As he toils, a man-made Prometheus, bound
   To the rail instead of the rock.
The coward, he dare not slip from the line,
   That is guiding his feet beneath,
For his soul would burst from him in gushes of flame,
   Like a sword drawn in haste from its sheath.

So a trust without doubt in the lines leading out
   The sinewy sweep of his length,

Keeps him still to their grasp, **though** his vigour within
Fain would lift him in frolic of strength.
Ah, me ! could I so keep true to my life,
And the good that would fain lead me on,
And turn my breast, like his own great chest,
To the war we must battle alone.

But this thought sinks **away as I** ask in my fear,
Will he never halt in his speed,
But rush onward and shriek his **wild watchword,** " Go on,
Like the Jew in the legend we read ?
No. Far in the distance, in front of his goal,
Falls down a finger of red,
And with a death-rattle of **one wild snort**
His flame-tortured spirit **is dead.**

And look ; **can that** fellow, just five feet eight,
With scarce a beard on his chin,
Can he, **too,** snatch at the slacks of the rein,
Till he groans as he tightens him in ?
He can. And this Vulcan of smoke and flame,
With such a momentum of will,
Stands at last a grim smoky colossus in steel,
And two rail-lengths of muscle is still.

Ay, call **me, the** sneer lying deep on **your lip,**
The paler but cultured ape ;
Lord of the brute, with the soul of a brute,
And a cunning to fashion and shape.
I turn from your creed to this miracled **deed**
We have set on twin pathways **of rods ;**
And I know that the new flings a blush on the old,
And that my fellows are gods.

BERTHA.

BERTHA grew up to noble womanhood
Full of the light of smiles, and in her eyes,
As sweet as spring flowers in their solitude,
Grew into bud and bloom her sympathies.

Then love came knocking at her gentle heart,
  And gave a sweeter colour to her cheek,
While far within new thoughts began to start
  Whose whispers made her smile but never speak.

For Bertha had this task her life before—
  To cheer her poor blind mother, and to guide
Her failing footsteps round the cottage door,
  And **read** God's word to her at eventide.

This **in her** purity she held above
  All others in the bounds of human ties ;
And in the light of this sweet task of love
  Grew she up, noble, beautiful, and wise.

No stir was in her life—the happy days,
  Like great white clouds within **a** summer sky,
Crept slowly on, and left continual praise
  In her sweet heart, and peace that could not die.

And still at all the task she held so dear,
  And in the splendour of her filial choice,
She seem'd an angel sent from heaven to cheer
  Her mother with the music of her voice.

Ah me ! what melody lay in its tone,
  When, in **the** quiet of the twilight dim,
She sang, her mother's hand within her own,
  The simple worship of their evening hymn.

Oft have **I** paused to hear its tender sounds,
  Awe-struck, as when within some pure, fair breast
A spirit song, escaping heavenly bounds,
  Creeps, hushing all the soul to perfect rest.

Thus **have** I stood in silent ecstasy,
  With all my daily **rougher life away,**
And in my heart the **wish to** bend my knee,
  When Bertha bow'd her golden head to pray.

But when she knelt in all her radiant youth,
  Pure as her sister angels far above,

My heart found its own worship in the truth,
  And reverence for all her trust and love.

So, Bertha, knowing it not, with quiet will
  Works in this life of mine, and with sweet tone
Speaks in my heart's own hours of calm, and still
  My spirit trembles to be like her own.

Thanks, Bertha, for this better life in me,
  Thanks for this reverence for all good below,
Thanks for thy yearning love and purity
  That stamps God's mission on thy noble brow.

THE MOTHER.

ONE night, returning from my work, I saw
  A woman standing by the churchyard gate,
And in her eyes a look of solemn awe
  And sadness, such as comes to mortal state
When the heart loses, by one sudden touch,
Its all on earth, or what is held as such.

I paused a moment, for I thought if she
  Was there a mourner for the dead who lie
In such sweet sleep, it were a sin in me
  To mar with idle step the sanctity
Of all her tears and wishes, for I ween
A woman's sorrow never should be seen.

So, with a footstep suited to her thought
  And the still place, I pass'd her, but askance
I stole a look when she could see me not—
  Grief seldom sees—and, following the glance
Of her tear-dimm'd and earnest-gazing eyes,
I saw a fresh new grave of tiny size.

And then it struck me that, three days before,
  A little one, aweary with the dearth
Of joys upon this cold, unfeeling shore,
  Had left with angels for a brighter earth—

Where the long day hath never tears nor sleep,
And this was the pale mother come to weep.

I could not check the sudden tears that came,
  Brought by the fancy that within its cell
The little one would have in death the same
  All kindred love and instinct that could tell
Its mother kept a tender watch above,
And so would tremble to return her love.

So all that evening, sitting by the fire,
  I still could see the mother, pale and wan,
With the great love within that nought could tire,
  From Nature and her all-mysterious plan,
Standing a pale, meek, earnest worshipper,
Over the little dust so dear to her.

O sacred grief, O deep and yearning love,
  The very type of God's! I raise my eyes
In feeble worship to the sky above,
  Beaming with stars, and bless those dear sweet ties
That lift us from this earth and our own clay,
Nearer to the Almighty and His day!

TASSO.

ALL pale by the dungeon door he stands,
  His own sweet sky above,
And he holds a book in his trembling hands,
  The labour of years and love.

And, lo, as he opens that single book,
  As if by some holy ray,
The dungeon shadows grow pale in look
  And forever pass away.

They pass away from the dull, drear cell
  To give place to a spirit sweet,
Who paces its floor as the ages swell
  With sweetly sounding feet.

And wherever their sound has the power to reach,
  They come of the kindred mind
Like pilgrims to hear that spirit preach
  Which the poet has left behind.

From many a distant and colder land
  They come and in silence look,
And see by the dungeon the poet stand
  Still clasping that single book.

They enter in, and the cell grows bright
  As the wings of the cherubim,
While the footsteps grow soft, and sweet, and light,
  Like leaves at their evening hymn.

They bow, and their spirit is not alone,
  For swift from the calm past years
The dead man's being strikes full on their own,
  And their heart grows big with tears.

O wonderful unseen power that still
  As the ages roll along
Heaps scorn on the tyrant's might and will,
  But deifies endless song.

THE RED LEAF.

HAVE you so forgot the time, dear love,
  When we sat by the stream in the wood
With our hearts as bright as the sky above,
  Talking as lovers should?
And we whisper'd to each of that happy day—
  Looking forward is so sweet—
But still as the moments sped away
  The red leaf fell at our feet.

The birds were out on the leafy boughs,
  Strong in their voice and youth,
And between their songs we made our vows
  With a kiss to seal their truth;

And I turn'd to you as I said, " This stream"—
    The stream was then so sweet—
" Has music fit for our coming dream,"
    And the red leaf fell at our feet.

The blushes lay warm on your gentle cheek,
    As I took your hand in mine,
While your eyes they could not, would not speak
    Aught but that love of thine ;
And you smiled as I clasp'd and kiss'd you still—
    Your smile was then so sweet—
But ever between the joy and thrill
    The red leaf fell at our feet.

I took the curls of your long, rich hair,
    And nursed them in my hand,
As we laid in the future clear and fair,
    The dreams we both had plann'd ;
We had nothing to do with life's alloy—
    O the heart will rise and beat—
But still as we spoke of our coming joy
    The red leaf fell at our feet.

We stood by the gate as the virgin night
    Set her footsteps on the hill,
Yet so sweet was your eyes with their dark rich light,
    That I fondly linger'd still ;
But hours wait not whatever we do,
    And lovers' hours are sweet,
So I kiss'd you again and said, " Be true,"
    And the red leaf lay at our feet.

Now I walk this life with a solemn brow,
    For the sweetest of hopes is fled,
And the blossoms that once would burst and blow
    Are now for ever dead.
Yet I smile as they question " Why is this ?"—
    O the pain of the inward heat !—
And seem to be gay as I laugh and say,
    The red leaf fell at our feet.

SUMMER DREAMINGS.

THERE seems a moving life to-day
  In everything I see,
The stream that laughs and leaps away,
  The grass beside the tree ;

The birds that, like to some swift thought,
  Flash through the sweet green boughs,
And pay in every leafy spot
  The music of their vows ;

The clouds, too, resting on the hill,
  Seem to my dreaming eye
Like angels coming to us still
  With pardon from on high.

And as I clasp all this at once,
  And feeling no alloy,
I teach my heart to give response
  To each sweet call of joy.

So, dreaming idly as I sit,
  And idly dreaming see
The sunny landscape wink and flit
  In silent ecstacy :

I think that all that can rejoice
  This long sweet summer day
Hath power to frame a gentle voice,
  And sing in love away.

So from the wood, and from the grass,
  And from the shady tree
Words come that like to whispers pass,
  Yet all are known to me.

And smiling as I catch their truth,
  I build upon their lore
A world again, and give it youth,
  And love, and something more.

But doubts will warp themselves through all,
　　And each bright vision rears
A fairy temple but to fall,
　　And leave me to my tears.

Now strange that from such dreams should rise
　　Such shadows to betray
The summer brightness of the skies,
　　And dull this breathing day.

Yet I might know that Nature still
　　Will work and work alone,
And will not blend her perfect skill
　　With what she must disown.

THE OLD LOVE LIVING YET.

THERE are some things still in this life of ours
　　The years weed not away,
But reverse the fate of dying flowers,
　　And bloom but in decay.
So I look back through the many years
　　Whose suns have long since set,
And feel, like the coming up of tears,
　　The old love living yet.

O the heart will wither up, when youth
　　Withdraws its fleeting light,
And think no more with the same sweet truth
　　That fed it day and night;
But amid the wreck of all we see,
　　And the cares that come and fret,
It will keep a bud from the blighted tree
　　Of the old love living yet.

There gathers still, like a mighty thought,
　　Around that magic name,
All the beating of a heart that brought
　　Its strength to one sweet aim;

And the flush and warmth of those early dreams—
    Ah, what heart could e'er forget !
Will waken up like the sun's first beams
    At the old love living yet.

So I think, as a dying light is toss'd
    From the gladness seen behind,
That whatever we in our youth have lost
    But models the future mind ;
And I weep as I think how my hopes may fall
    Like the leaves when the winds are met,
And leave in my heart a scorn for all
    Save the old love living yet.

ON THE ENGINE IN THE NIGHT-TIME.

ON the engine in the night-time, with the darkness all around,
And below the iron pulses beating on with mighty sound.
  And I stand as one in wonder, till within a flush of pride
Leaps and kindles, and my soul is in the mighty monster's stride.
Then I hear amid the clanking and the tumult of the steel,
Something like a song spring upward from the grinding of the
    wheel,
Low at first, but high and higher till, as day is wide and free,
Came the song, and this mad lyric sang the monster unto me :—
" In the glowing of my bosom, in the roar and rush of fire,
Is the strength that makes the distance shrivel in to my desire,
And I roll along in thunder swift as is the lightning fleet—
Let the Frankensteins who made me keep the guiding of my feet,
For I work with them and labour, bearing in my smoky mirth
All the strain and rush of traffic, as an Atlas bears the earth ;
Striving with them till my sinews, bending to their mighty load,
Shake and glisten like the muscles on the shoulder of a god.
Shame that I should let such puppets move me at their slightest
    will—
I, the Cyclops of this darkness, with a forehead flaming still—
I who have within a vigour equal to all fabled pow'r,
And the soul of mad Prometheus, with his cunning for a dow'r !
But they draw me onward, placing iron threads to meet my grasp,
Linking all my strength to method and a hundred-armèd clasp,

So that all my panting being, marvelling at such display,
Questions, as I foam and thunder, 'Who is greater? I or they?'
This should gall me, but their purpose mixing ever with my own,
Keeps the iron will within me pulsing to a proper tone.
Therefore let my mission widen till my shriek of triumph rings,
Ever from the front of Progress rushing on through human things.
Lo! the ages yet that slumber in the mighty womb of Time,
At their birth shall gather round me, for my strength shall touch
    its prime.
They shall take me for their pulse, and bring around my giant life
All the mad and restless world, with its myriad forms of strife.
Then a deeper thirst shall stir me, and a wilder vigour cling
To my never tiring sinews, as my iron footsteps ring.
Puppets of a restless frenzy, they shall work me till the earth
Bears upon her furthest bosom fiery tokens of my birth.
But I make myself a prophet, yet these miracles shall be,
And be sung in lyrics worthy of this iron heart in me.
Therefore thou who standest wondering while I toil and shriek
    along,
See that all my world mission touch thee into proper song.
Sing the nerve and toil within me, and the vast desires that fret,
Till before them all their purpose and their mighty goals are set ;
Sing them unto men in music, rough as is my tortured shriek,
When my strength flares up within me, and my mighty soul must
    speak,
So that I may hear their pæans as I flash and thunder on,
The rough Hercules of Labour, ever potent and alone."

Thus the monster sang, and ever as he sped with flash and glare
All his fiery thoughts went upward, like red stars into the air,
And each throb that shook his being found a ready voice in mine,
Crying—All the soul within him is but as a part of thine ;
Then a deeper pride grew in me, and my heart beat higher still,
For I felt myself a part of all his iron strength and will—
Mine the endless grasp of sinew, mine the miracle of mind,
Mine the glory and the triumph of my toiling fellow-kind.
Thus I thought ; and through the night-time, as the monster
    clank'd along,
I grew prouder of my labour and my little gift of song.

BOOKS.

" The beings of the mind are not of clay ;
    Essentially immortal, they create
    And multiply in us a brigher ray,
      And more beloved existence."—*Childe Harold.*

" Un bon livre est un bon ami."—*B. de Saint Pierre.*

I have a little world within my home—
A world that cannot die though ages roam ;
For thought is king, and, with eternal sway,
Rules on while earthly monarchs pass away.
Change cannot touch him, and the dust that springs
From dull Time's duller footsteps never clings
To dim the glitter of his brow, but bright
It shines for ever, and can feel no night.

A world it is in which, with open looks
(I call them friends, but others call them books),
Are ministers that, at a moment's wish,
Pour forth their treasures with a quiet gush
Into the heart, until their gentle balm
Spreads round, and scatters universal calm.

There our own Shakespeare, with a mightier wand
Than ever his own wise Prospero could command,
Wakes from their slumbers all the mighty great
That shook a kingdom or could rule a State ;
Infuses life into each silent form,
And places each to move in calm and storm.
What power the mighty master had, to frame
A vanish'd time, and make it breathe the same !
From the fool's babble to the kingly throne
He moves, the enchanter of such space, alone.

Who comes, in Learning's silent chambers nursed,
A second Homer, blind as was the first ?
Milton, the Cyclops of a darkness given,
To fit his harp to sing of hell and heaven.
Hear him, and let all other lyres be mute.
" Of man's first disobedience, and the fruit,

Sing, Heavenly Muse ;" and sing, O, sing again
The earthly love that sire's a heavenly strain.

Next, dwarf'd in figure, but of giant brain,
Comes Pope, the stinger in heroic strain.
Where'er he moves his vigour follows still,
Which even in little things must show its skill.
Whether he steals a lady's tress, or hurls
A hundred would-be poets, with their curls,
Into oblivion, he is still the same,
The dreaded cut-throat that can stab a name.
He moves in might, and I must read his strains,
To feel myself a dunce for all my pains.
What wondrous puppet show is this I see ?
A hundred Lilliputs around my knee,
Moving so real and life-like to my view,
I never ask myself, " Can this be true ?"
Who moves the wires that guide these little things ?
A master perfect in the heart's deep springs—
A lone old man, whose worn and tortured breast
Knew every passion save the high and best.
I will not smile, but let the pageant glide,
And weep for genius when it steps aside.

What noise is this I hear, and broken words
That seem to sound like guns and drums and swords ?
'Tis Uncle Toby and his worthy Trim,
Talking of sieges and of horrors grim.
I will not speak, but let the couple pass,
While Widow Wadman stands before the glass
Touching her beauty, with a matron's art,
To gull my Uncle Toby's simple heart.

Who steps before me next with smiling brow,
And bosom beating with fraternal glow ?
Why, Parson Adams ; and he shakes my hand
So kindly, as we both together stand,
Then, all unwitting of my presence near,
Draws out his Æschylus he holds most dear,
Begins to read, and so I gently speak,
" Good Parson Adams, I have not the Greek."

He puts away the book, and asks the lend
Of half-a-crown—it is to help a friend.
I give it to him, and, as he departs,
I bless the simple Parson's simple arts.

With jaunty bearing and affected mien,
Who comes in haste to fill the changing scene ?
Beau Tibbs, and with him, too, the grave Chinese,
Who writes to Fum Hoam what he hears and sees.
Beau Tibbs espies me, and, with studied tact,
Hastens a sudden friendship to contract,
Talks much of Wakefield's Vicar, and I budge
A step or two away, and mutter " Fudge !"
Invites me to his house, which I decline ;
" Your time is short," he says, " and so is mine.
Good-bye." He waves a brisk salute, and stalks
Away to wander in his favourite walks.

Furrow'd in brow, and beard as white as snow,
Yet eye that glitters with a youthful glow,
Comes one whom I at once pronounce to be
The Mariner, to tell his tale to me.
What care I for his ship in tropic day ?
I will not hear him, but will slip away.
In vain ; he holds me, and, with wizard skill,
Tells on his tale—" the Mariner hath his will."

O for a wing of mighty flight to fly
And view Lake Leman with Childe Harold's eye,
Catch all at once the sunny space of sea,
And feel its inspiration rise to me ;
Walk in the spirit with that mighty mind
Who drew the gloomy bosoms of his kind
Till calumny, with narrow serpent view,
Whisper'd he sat himself for what he drew,
And foul suspicion, ever prone to fill
Shadow with substance, haunts his spirit still !

With child-like features, and a wondering look
Bent evermore upon an open'd book,
Comes Shelley, clear and cold in that high faith
Which is not for this world nor human breath,

K

But some far fairy clime.   He speaks, and lo !
I talk with Julian and Madalo,
Lie with Prometheus upon the rock,
And for a moment brave the vulture's shock,
Then mourn for Adonaïs—he who sung
The Pagan wonders when the world was young,
Or shudder at the Cenci's awful mind,
And all the demon madness there design'd—
But hush ! he passes on to meet the wild
Deep waters and become the " eternal child."

What grey-hair'd man is this who sits and sees
His dogs around him gambol at their case ?
'Tis Scott, the wizard, who can charm all time
With lays of minstrels and rough Border rhyme ;
Shakespeare in prose, he lifts his magic wand,
And lo ! beneath the skill at his command,
Kings start and mighty warriors, till we feel
Our spirit breathing in an age of steel,
And pant and glow to join the tourney's shock,
When lances splinter and the chargers rock.
See Wilfred, with Rowena by his side,
Rebecca drooping in her maiden pride,
Cedric, and Wamba with his jesting art,
De Bracy, Richard of the lion heart,
Bold Robin Hood, exempt from every law,
Twanging his merry bow in " greenwoode schawe,"
Stern Front de Bœuf.   These pass and leave their room
To others bright in robe and gay in plume—
Leicester, sweet Amy, England's frigid Queen,
Our hapless Mary, bright in beauty's mien,
Dark Ravenswood, rough Burley, great Dundee,
Vich Ian Vohr, Prince Charles, high and free,
Captain Dirk Hatternick, and Meg Merrilees,
The Dominie, all agape at what he sees,
Who, as he moves his lank and learnèd frame,
Shouts out " Pro-di-gi-ous," and I do the same.

Who would not bless and praise the humorous skill
Of he who with a sketch can tickle still ?—
Dickens, whose fertile brain has given to Time
(Time gets such gifts that makes him all sublime)

Sam Weller, Peggoty, that **honest life,**
John Peerybingle, Dot, his little wife;
Meek, patient Agnes, in her **purity**
Of thought and life—thus should fair woman be.
O bright **creations** that for ever rise
Before **us, claiming** all our sympathies,
Eternal in their youth they cannot die,
But, soul-like, live in immortality.

Who sings the upright Arthur and his time
In purest English and in clearest rhyme?
'Tis he who wears the laurel none **can** claim
Until their lyres are fit to sound the same.
I see gay Lancelot, tough at sword and spear;
He bows, and looks askance on Guinevere;
And naughty Vivien, **what** a mess you made
Of poor old Merlin in the woodland shade;
Elaine, **still** pining all her truth to prove,
Brave Geraint, Enid **in her** patient love;
And last, King Arthur, **ere** he joins the strife,
Bending above his prostrate, guilty wife,
Half stern in ire, yet wishing naught to **prove,**
She owning all, as to win back his love.
These fade away, but to return when I
Am all alone, and wish their presence nigh;
They **come** unchanged, for years make ever bright
The forms that genius gives to thought and light.

O glorious books, whose silent-worded leaves
Have balm for cypress'd Sorrow when she grieves;
Smiles for fair Hope, and worn and drooping Care;
Flowers for the gloom that lies before Despair—
Our friends **are** ye, that through all good and ill
Keep your sweet faiths the same to cheer us still,
Filling our solitude with shapes and things
That wait upon us with their ministerings,
Serene and calm in their own quiet art;
They touch us, and we clasp them heart-to-heart,
Until their being knits itself to ours,
And half our own is given to grace their pow'rs,
Twin'd to their friendship, which we hold above
All **others,** since it cannot change its love.

I MISS MY BONNIE BAIRN.

MISS my bonnie bairn,
   I miss him unco sair,
I miss him stan'in' at the door,
   I miss him up the stair,
I miss the patter o' his feet
   That toddled out an' in,
But O, I miss him warst ava'
   When the day's wark is dune.

Then John sits by the fire,
   An', though he disna speak,
I ken fu' weel his thocht,
   For the tears are on his cheek.
The tears grow big upon his cheek,
   An' my ain begin to fa',
As my heart still murmurs on—
   Your twa years' bairn's awa'.

An' just yestreen I chanced,
   When townin' through the drawer,
To come upon his plaiks laid by,
   Their sicht but made me waur.
For there the wee toy-horsie lay
   I had tae let him see
An' hour afore death cam' an' took
   The licht frae oot his e'e.

Weel, weel, I min' that nicht
   His faither brocht it in,
I took it to his wee bedside
   An' touch'd him on the chin—
"Come, look up, Jamie, my big man,
   An' see this bonnie sicht."
He raise, an' took it frae my han',
   An' O, his e'e was bricht!

Prood was I when I saw that look,
   An' John was unco fain;

I keekit in his face, an' speer'd,
  What think ye o' the wean ?
He'll live an' bless us a', **if ance**
  This **tout he** warstles through ;
For I like the glegness o' his look,
  An' the smile aboot his **mou'.**

But waes me, **or** an hour gaed by,
  Death hush'**d** him safe an' soun ;
An' a' oor hopes fell ow'r **his face,**
  As winter leaves fa' doon.
But they'll a' grow fresh an' green **again,**
  Tho' noo I've this to learn,
The earth has to me ae dear spot—
  The wee grave o' **my bairn.**

AH! THE DREAMS.

A H ! the dreams that I had from the poet,
  When my soul drank in his song,
Have pass'd away with their splendour,
  As the sunlight sweeps along.

And I feel no more the magic,
  And the fancies of rainbow glow
That forever were with **me** and **in me**
  In those years of long ago.

Yet I sigh for those early **visions**
  As a bird longs for its mate ;
Or as fields for the rain in summer ;
  But I weary as I wait.

For I feel that my heart is empty,
  That the chambers within it must,
For lack **of their old** sweet dwellers,
  Grow **dim and** gather dust.

Then come, O, ye vanish'd sunbeams,
   That fell from the higher truth ;
And come, O, ye aspirations
   That peal'd through the march of youth.

Take your home in my heart's still chambers,
   Let your footsteps be on the floor,
Till the smiles of your joy and gladness
   Make this earth as it was before.

But they come no more to cheer me
   As they did in those early days,
When the earth like a mighty temple
   Flew open with psalm and praise.

They have left my rough, firm manhood
   To colder and harsher gleams,
And have flown to some younger bosom
   Aflush with its first sweet dreams.

But I mourn for that fallen worship
   That will never rise again,
And my life droops at times with a sadness
   As if of foreshadow'd pain.

Ah, the griefs that are in this lifetime
   Seem but shadows to those that come
When the temples within us crumble,
   And our first sweet faiths grow dumb.

ADA.

LYING full-length upon the summer grass,
   And by the murmur of a summer stream,
I heard the village bell, and turning round
To him who sat beside me with his feet
Touching the ripple of the brook, I said,
" Who sinks into the churchyard rest to-day ?"

Then he, half lifting up his earnest face,
Paused for a little while, and then replied—
" Ada, whose beauty was a fairy thing,
But brighter now by death, whose pencil tints
His marks with such sweet colours."

     Then he sunk
Into that dreamy reverie which **shuts**
All thought from **out its vision, and so thinks,**
And thinks, and thinks, and yet thinks naught at all ;
But I, half-answer'd, could but ill abide
His silentness, and so I question'd still :
" But who is Ada **?** you have **never** said,
And there you dream, and think, and all the while
The tolling of the bell within my ear,
And yet I know not unto whom it offers
Such sweet and stirless rest."

     Then starting up
From all his fit of mute philosophy
He said, " Why, surely you have not forgot
Ada, who flash'd upon you like a star
Three months ago, when you were in the woods,
At your old rambles, and she knew it not,
But pass'd you in her beauty by, and you
Fell half in love with her and writ a song ?"

Then **all at** once came, like remember'd **dreams,**
The solitude around the woodland **walk,**
And **all** the fringing of the idle rhyme
(Now something better by the help of Death),
Which I had made in haste, and sung **to him**
A half-hour after. Now, what better time
Than this, I cried, to sing that song again,
When she is passing from all mortal view
Into the shady quietness. And he,
Catching the broader **finish** of the plan,
Said, " Let the song be sung, but make a pause
Between each stanza, that the bell may chime
Its echoes at the finish of each verse,
And let your poet's fancy shape the words."

So, with the humming idyll of the brook
As an accompaniment I sang the song :

Ada came down by the path in the wood,
  In the flush and the warmth of the day,
And the spirits that live in the solitude
  (For there be such they say)
Came out from their haunts by tree and brook,
  And wherever sunbeams play,
To gaze, as she pass'd like a bud on the lake—
A sweet Diana of earthly make—
  In the clasp of the amorous day.

I ceased, and the sad bell took up the pause,
And sang an answer to its solemn chime :

Ada walks no earthly path,
  Other things are hers this hour ;
She has all an angel hath—
  Glory and celestial pow'r ;
Nought may look on her but eyes
  Purged from aught of mortal sight,
  As she walks in balmy light
In the halls of Paradise.
  So the dust may shrink, but she
Through the years, in the spheres,
  Is one great type of immortality.

So sang the bell, and when its echo died
I took my part in turn, and sang again :

I was out in the wood when she pass'd me by,
  Half-hid that she could not see,
So a woman's wish was in her eye,
And a smile that made me, I know not why,
  Guess and dream that she
Was far away in the golden hope
  Of the coming time, and the novel scope
Of wifehood, and the prattling bliss
  Of little lips, and this, and this
Was the light and colour within her eye,
  And the smile as she pass'd me by.

Then sang the bell, more solemn than before,
Its critic strictures on my little song :—

Hush ! for angels may not speak
   Mother in her ear to-day—
She so bright, and pure, and meek,
   What has she to do with clay ?
Past and present things are o'er,
   Custom cannot come to her,
She has nothing now in store
   But the task of worshipper,
And the short frivolous world is hers no more.

Thus sang the bell, and when it ceas'd we rose
And took the pathway by the streamlet's edge
(The seal of fitting silence on our lips),
Then he, striking across the meadows to his home,
Left me in silence to walk on to mine,
Deep in a strange sweet thought.   All the way I mused
On this dread death.   I heard the gentle stream
Sing to itself—saw all the wild sweet flowers
That look up to us full of love and trust—
Heard far on either side the birds that strain'd
Their songs, full-throated, sending everywhere
A flood of song ; and each and all had looks
Of some high mystery, but were so full
Of their own life they would or could not tell.
So in half-whispers to myself I said,
" This death is but a slight gloom-shaded door,
Set like a niche within the wall of life,
And those that enter in turn slowly round
And shut it, and we hear the sound.   But that
Which comes to each within the lonely rooms
Is seal'd until we enter, led by Death.
Nor do they come again, save unto those
Who, strong in grief as in the power to shape,
Can bring them back, bath'd in a shower of tears,
And baffle death a moment,   Thus with me
And right before me in the narrow path
Ada rose up as fair and sweet as when
She lightly stept throughout the green sweet woods
Humming a little song to suit her thought ;

Nor did she leave me till I pass'd the wall
Of the old churchyard, stept across the bridge
And turn'd the corner of the little street,
And laid my hand upon our humble door.

THE SPIRIT OF THE TIMES.

COME, fling for a moment, my fellows,
  The pick and shovel aside,
And rise from the moil of our ten hours' toil
  With a heart beating high with pride.
What though our mission can do without thought,
  And the music and cunning of rhymes ;
Yet shame on that bosom that will not throb
  To the spirit and march of the times.

Then, hurrah ! for this rough, firm earth of ours,
  Like a lion half-roused from his den
She wakes, and cries, while we whisper in fear,
  " Let us hush her to sleep again."
But a voice from the very footstool of God
  Cries, ' Break her away from her thrall,
That our fellows may toss her from hand to hand.
  As a juggler tosses his ball."

Come, then, let us thunder our watchword still,
  " Make way for the tools and the man,"
Let the rough hand work what the thought will shape
  To its highest miraculous plan—
Till the gods, who loll at the edge of the stars,
  Look down as we labour below,
And swear by their nectar these puppets beneath
  They know how their planet should go.

Fling the span of the bridge o'er the foam of the sea,
  Run shafts to the centre of earth,
Wrench the coal from her grasp to the light of the sun,
  That the giant of steam may have birth.

Lay the pliant rail on her full broad breast,
  That, swift as a lion springs,
The engine may hurtle and roar—the Danton
  Of this wondrous new birth of things !

Build the ship into being from stem to stern,
  But not with wood as of yore,
But with iron plates that may laugh at the shock
  Of the thunder hammer of Thor.
Let the sea swell up in his white-lip'd wrath,
  As the circling paddles fly,
And Neptune himself groan for want of room
  Till the iron hulk goes by.

O, fellows, but this is a wondrous age,
  When Science springs up from her bars,
And shoots in her thirst from this planet of ours
  To the very front of the stars.
And we—we watch her as on she glides
  Leaving wonders behind her track,
Like a huntsman that jerks a hawk from his wrist,
  But who will whistle her back ?

Ay, who ; for at length she has found her strength,
  As a tiger's may come at the sup
Of the warm first blood, and his wild fierce mood
  Like fire through his frame flashes up ;
So she, and we follow as onward she leads
  With the flush of pride on her cheek,
And she makes us the greater man, though we work
  In the wake of the Roman and Greek.

Shame rest on the bigot that thinks in his heart
  She flings a blight on our creeds,
And darkens the light that we keep to guide
  As we rush from the fable to deeds.
Out on such croakers ! with one white hand
  She lifts her miracle rod
And strikes wherever we wish, while the other
  Holds on by the garments of God.

The ages behind look like infants in sleep,
  But those that look down on our time

Cry out with a hundred voices in one
  To nourish them into prime.
And, God ! but we build them up to their strength,
  As an eagle will rear her young,
But their giant force, springing up like a source,
  Has never yet been sung.

Where shall he come from, the poet,
  That shall place on his wild, rough page
The spirit that lurks and forever works
  In the breast of this mighty age ?
Is he yet in the cycles that loom before,
  Preparing his melody ?
Let him come, and roll through my heart and soul
  His music before I die.

But now while we wait for the roll of his words
  Let us work in our growing strength ;
For the earth in her cradle, since Adam died,
  Is up from her slumber at length.
Ay, up ! in the cities that roar and fret
  With the toil and the tread of men ;
And the sun shall be hurl'd from his course ere she sinks
  To her second childhood again !

Then, hurrah ! for our higher fellows that work
  With this thought and its Titan pow'rs,
And cut through the jungle of creeds and fools
  A path for this planet of ours.
And hurrah for this nineteenth century time—
  What the future may grow and be !
Ah, God ! to burst up from the slumber of death
  For one wild moment to see !

ONE OF THE FOUR IN SONG.

DOWN the vista of the fading years,
    With solemn step and slow,
Comes one whose brow is dim with inward tears
    And long unspoken woe.

Behind him factions with their evil look
    Struggle and hiss and cry ;
He turns at times with haughty front to brook
    Their insults with reply.

Before him in the purer calmer air
    The Muses glide and swim,
Holding a simple wreath all fresh and fair,
    That seems to be for him.

He stretches out his hand as if to grasp
    The laurel, but they cry—
Not yet shall this thy furrow'd brows enclasp,
    Wait, wait until thou die.

He passes slowly on till from the swell
    And echo of the throng
A voice cries Lo! the man that strode through hell
    And came out firm and strong.

Then with a heart within me beating fast,
    Knowing the poet now—
Dante, I whisper, and on me at last
    He turns his weary brow.

But that which in me rose up to be said
    Grows dumb before his look,
And, trembling in my fear, I bow my head
    As if at some rebuke.

But while I bow, his footsteps pass away ;
    And when I look again,
Lo, far off, in the purer, brighter day
    He stands without his pain :

And on his brow the Muses place the wreath
   He held so dear and sweet ;
Then joining fair white hands in tender faith,
   Kneel down and clasp his feet.

So stands he in his own all sunny clime
   That did him such great wrong ;
So stands he unto all for earthly time,
   One of the four in song.

UNDERNEATH THE STARS.

" L'amor che muove il Sole e l'altre stelle."—Dante.

I HAVE flung away my Dante, weary with the sounding line,
And the sad and solemn music of the mighty Florentine ;
  And I come out to the doorway with a throbbing in my heart
For the mission of the poet and his high and holy art.
But such gift is for the mighty who have rear'd in pain and tears
Finger-posts to guide the world moaning with its birth of years.
Giants who have heard in prisons, bolted by a tyrant's nod,
In their hearts like angel music footsteps of their guiding god.
Theirs is the melodious whisper floating in the front of time,
Bending human hearts and footsteps to the purpose in their chime.
But for me is no cool laurel, but the use that labour brings,
With a quiet voice at midnight harping on the lower strings.
Then I look up to the stars that beam and sparkle far above,
Soft, as whispers in my bosom, rises up their tender love.
Even as I stand and watch them, in their space so far away,
Down their shafts of light run whispers, and those whispers seem
   to say—
" O, thou lone one from thy chamber, weary with the toil of books,
Come and rest thyself a moment underneath our quiet looks—
Come and open up thy being till the silence all around
Be unto thy soul within a trembling realm of thoughtful sound.
Then I come out from the doorway, and the stars burn soft and
   sweet
As I turn my quiet footsteps up the lone and narrow street ;
Human hearts are all around me sleeping, as an infant sleeps,
Dreamless while my own between them still its busy vigil keeps.

Then I whisper, "O, my fellows, light be all thy slumbers now,
Voiceless lives are thine, yet noble in the labour on thy brow.
Then I pass the bridge and churchyard, with its dead in perfect rest,
Ah, what love springs up within me, filling all my alter'd breast;
For they come, the fair young dead, who in the early blush and strife
Wither'd, leaving all their perfume to come up behind my life;
Sweet as summer winds come back their heart-breath'd blessings
    unto me—
Love is love when from the grave the dead stretch out their hands
    to thee.
Then I turn to watch the river moaning in a broken dream,
Lo! a world of stars beneath me lies within its placid beam.
Stars above and stars beneath me standing thus between their
    pow'r,
Let my thoughts range into order and take colour from this hour.
First come all those inspirations, thronging through my passionate
    youth,
As through sculptors' dreams a vision to be set in marble truth.
Then the frets and fancies touching as with some magician's rod,
Dreams within the fair to-morrow to the brightness of a god.
Then the long melodious whisper filling every pause of time
With its flowing out of passion and its bursts of golden rhyme.
Then the grief for one fair being wither'd in the early bloom,
With its yellow madness sneering at the purpose of a tomb.
Shame on all that restless worship of the grand but aimless past,
Let the stars pour down their wisdom that this night may be its
    last.
Lo, from all their beams above me, from the shadows seen below,
Love comes to me, slowly filling all my being with its glow.
Love for Him that lit their lustre, love for human work and weal,
Love for all the wider space in which the heart must move and feel.
Then I bow as if my forehead felt the touch of spirit hands,
Bow and feel my better nature growing as a bud expands;
Then the silence all around me whispers with a fruitful sound—
Let the faith this night hath given keep thee ever in its bound.
Then I turn from stream and churchyard, pace again the little street,
All the old life dead within me, and the new life soft and sweet:
Feeling that this new existence must forever follow me,
Growing wider in the yearning and the trust in good to be,
Until like the soul of Dante it flings off its earthly bars,
Leaps from clay and clasps its arms around the sun, and moon, and
    stars.'

GIVE ME A SONG, THOU POET.

THE heart of the toiling world
    Shook with such sudden wrong
That it cried in its wrath to the poet—
    Poet, give me a song.

For the strong swift years uplabour,
    They shake me where I am weak ;
I am strong in the thoughts and purpose,
    But have not power to speak.

I thunder from triumph to triumph,
    But I crush as I roll along,
And whenever my glory gathers
    There is sure to be some wrong.

Then give me a song, thou poet,
    A lyric to fit that time
When love shall be one with labour,
    And both be held sublime.

And the earnest poet watching,
    Saw the throes of the toiling earth,
Heard its voice and the mighty yearning,
    And he knew what gave it birth.

So he open'd his prophet bosom,
    As he stood by the stream alone,
And a song burst from the poet,
    And the world made it its own.

THE DEAD LARK.

ON the slope, half-hid in grass, and right beneath the sounding
    wire,
  Lay the lark, the sweetest singer in the Heavenly Father's
    choir,
Dead, no more to thrill the heavens with his music long and loud,
Coming from the sunny silence, moving on the fleecy cloud.
Tenderly the thing I lifted, smooth'd the ruffle on his breast,
That had still'd the beat of life and sent his singing soul to rest.
O, what melodies unutter'd, lyrics of the happiest praise,
Lay within my hands, forever useless to the summer days.
Then I thought a want would wander, like a strangely jarring tone
Through the singing choir, and only to be mark'd of God alone.
For we muffle up our vision, seeing not for earthly stain
All that He in wisdom fashions for His glory and our gain.
And as still I stood and held him, in the sunshine overhead
Sang and shook his merry fellows, heedless of their brother dead ;
Then my heart was stirr'd within me as I heard them at their song,
For I deem'd their touch of music did this little fellow wrong,
And my tears came slowly upward as a low sweet undertone
Whisper'd to me, " Thus for ever sing the thoughtless of thy own.
Far into the realms of fancy soar they in their sounding flight,
Heeding not below some brother with a wing of feebler might."
Yet the same sweet aspirations throb through all the songs he
    sings,
And the same deep impulse yearning for the better human things,
But his voice like sounds in twilight echoes but to die away,
While the deep heart throbbing in him fain would burst into the
    day.
But his higher fellows hear not, listen not its earnest tone
That comes out in simple sound between the pauses of their own,
So he pines away in silence, keeping back the tide of song,
Till the rush and fret within him works at last its end in wrong ;
And he, seeing beyond the promise of a better kindred band,
Dies, his bosom full of lyrics, like the lark's within my hand.

Waking up, the day's set labour still'd the fancies in my breast,
So I laid the fallen minstrel into his unnoticed rest,
Left him and the music with him lying in his grassy bed
To the carol of his fellows and the sunshine overhead.

THE POOL.

THE wind through the summer woods blows cool,
   So I walk with quiet pace,
But I stop a little at the pool,
   And again I see your face.

Just where the pale primroses peep
   Above the dimpling stream,
I see as in some magic sleep
   A form to suit my dream.

And bright, and warm, and sweet to view
   It grows distinct and fair,
As if the waves were mirrors true
   And you were looking there:

All just the same as you stood that day,
   When the wind was low and cool,
With your feet on the wild-flowers where they lay,
   And your shadow in the pool.

But I could not reach the one wild rose
   That in your hand was seen ;
For still as thought and act would close,
   The pool grew up between.

Ah heart, ah heart, I turn away
   From the dreams of my idle brain,
And sigh to think that this summer day
   Hath power to bring me pain ;

For how many things in my little life
   Have offer'd unto me
Their fresh sweet hopes with blossoms rife
   As the spring-buds on a tree.

But still as my hand would make display
   To gather what was seen,
Like the silent pool by the forest way
   A gap grew up between.

L U C Y.

LUCY is but a child as yet,
　And full of mirth and glee,
But still in Lucy's eye is set
　A light that I love to see.

For it speaks of the coming golden time,
　When, like April flowers in a wood,
She will blossom up into the happy prime
　Of innocent maidenhood.

Then the smile will be sweeter upon her lip,
　And brighter upon her brow,
And her heart take a sweeter dream and slip
　Into other thoughts than now.

This is their coming light that lies
　Like sunlight within the stream,
In the glowing depths of her large sweet eyes
　That droop at times to dream.

Ah me, what wishes such light will get
　To perfect into flower !
But Lucy is but a child as yet,
　Nor heeds her coming dower.

Then why should I touch her heart's sweet chords
　In my poet's mood, and try
To shape to the music of earthly words
　Their tender melody ?

I will leave this to the summer in bud,
　That unseen, in its sweetness, weaves
A glory to round her maidenhood,
　As the wind swells out the leaves.

But speak not to Lucy as yet of this,
　Though her eyes in their dreaming may,
And hint, as they droop, of their coming bliss,
　As the light foretells the day.

But let mirth be upon her lip and brow,
  And within her large dark eyes,
Till her own sweet thoughts that are budding now
  Waft her into her Paradise.

THE SUN.

Die Sonne tönt nach alter weise.—Goethe.

HE rises as of old, he flings
  A grandeur over earth and sea,
And life wakes up in lifeless things
  And bounds into fertility.
The earth upheaves her bosom, wet
  With fruitful tears, and in her veins
The myriad beat of life is set,
  And pulses with a thousand gains.

He rises as of old—the stars
  Shrink from his pathway, and their light
Fades back into the heaven that bars
  A glory from all mortal sight.
He sinks; and round his fiery track,
  Where the blue heaven meets above,
Their dazzling lustre eddies back,
  And fills the world with light and love.

He rises as of old—his race
  Is swifter than that angel's flight
Who flies in glory through the space
  Of stars to tell his master's might.
He wearies not—but upward springs,
  A wonder unto those below
Who walk beneath his purple wings,
  And live in their sustaining glow.

He rises as of old—the shade
  Of Him who, from the highest seat
Through the wild waste of chaos, made
  A pathway for his glowing feet;

Along this path, beneath His eye,
He thunders ; and, as on he swims,
The stars, within the boundless skies,
Attend him with harmonious hymns.

THE LARK.

A SPIRIT sang from the edge of a cloud
A wondrous melody.
O spirit, I whisper'd, half aloud,
Come down with that song to me ;

For I know that my own is poor and weak,
But if my heart was like thine
I could utter a sweeter music, and speak
Better thoughts to this world of mine.

Then I bow'd my head in the soft, green grass,
Three daisies beneath my face,
And listen'd to hear if the spirit would pass
From his cloud-propp'd dwelling-place.

And lo! from his home in the azure above
He came with his wondrous song,
And so deep was its melody dipp'd in love
That my heart beat quick and strong.

Nearer he came at each thrill of his mirth,
Till close beside me he dropp'd,
But as soon as his feet touch'd my own dull earth
The heaven-fed melody stopp'd.

Then, wild with a longing this spirit to see,
I raised my head from the dark,
And there, with his bright eyes looking at me,
Was the crested head of a lark.

THE UNCO BIT WEAN.

HER faither says aften fu' plainly to me,
"The wean, woman, 's juist like oor neebors, we see,
An' naething ava to mak siccan a sang
As ye dae aboot her a' the leevy day lang."
But I say to him, "Na, she's my ain wee bit tot,
An' has ways o' her ain that nae ithers hae got;"
An' as for himsel', losh, I'm gey far mistaen
If he disna think her just an unco bit wean.

For ye see when she first noticed things an' grew croose,
She wad follow him glegly through a' the hale hoose;
An' at nicht, when he cam' frae his wark, I declare,
Ye'd hae thocht that she ken'd his first step on the stair.
An' then when he half put his heid into sicht,
Cryin' " Keeky-bo, where's my wee Maggie the nicht?"
The wee thing could scarce keep her seat on my knee,
As he ran up like daft to kiss baith her an' me.

But noo when she's gotten the fit an' can rin,
What a flutter at times she can pit us baith in,
For she toddles a' gates, though her favourite feat
Is to climb up on chairs and look oot on the street;
An' if a big horse or a dog comes in sicht,
She jumps in sic glee that we rin, in oor fricht,
An' grup baith her legs, while her faither declares
That this same trick o' hers 'ill bring on his grey hairs.

Then, the taste that she has puzzles me warst ava,
An' yet her bit mou' never gie's the least thraw,
Though a waught o' saip suds an' a mouthfu' o' ink
She took ance unawares when in search o' a drink.
I hae seen her mysel' lyin' cantie an' droll
At a pic-nic o' cinders, drawn frae the ase-hole.
Bless the wean! what a lesson for fat epicures
Wha gang smackin' their lips through this warl' o' oors.

Then, in flooers I maun say that she tak's little pride;
For a big bunch o' grass, growin' by the roadside,

A lang dandelion, or docken fu' braid
Can pit a' your fine hot-house gems in the shade.
I whiles say, " Dear me, what an' odd kind o' wean,
Sae chock-fu' o' things that we canna explain ;"
But her faither hauds out, in his ain joky **way**,
She's the maist original wean o' her day.

Then at nicht when she **rows aboot in her nicht claes,**
She maun hae half an hour to get **countin'** her taes,
Or rinnin' aboot wi' sic bursts o' pure glee,
That her faither looks up half in wonner at **me ;**
But whenever I rise frae my chair to gie **chase**
She comes to my arms, an' sic laughin' tak's place,
That I'm thankfu' when Sleep comes to weave his mute spell,
An' **tak' a' her** thochts an' sweet dreams **to** himsel'.

She's oor tae ee, the wean, an' the licht in oor hame,
Through which, when we look, this life's no like the same,
But glows as if seen through the **shadow** of God,
Till again we hae Paradise in oor abode ;
An' we fill up wi' joy ow'r this wee bud o' oors
That, springlike, has put a' **oor ain** into flooers,
An' the bliss we hae in her can never depart,
For we **lie** doon at nicht wi' her lauch in oor heart.

J E A N I E.

ЧOU were dead, they said ;
  In the churchyard had been laid,
Many weeks ago, the dust whose youth was in its fullest **pride :**
  Simple words and simply spoken,
  Yet they struck me white with terror as **if** fiends had **flung a**
    token
  At my feet of my eternal doom, when all this life was broken,
And I slumber'd in the churchyard not a footstep from thy side
                    —Jeanie.

      More I could not ask,
      For I felt how ill the task

To check the tears that in my heart as yet were all **unseen.**
   I had come in all the gladness
   That will ever mark a youth whose love is in its first wild madness.
     O day that first grew high with hope, **and** now had so much sadness,
I could only **see the** doorway where thy footstep **once** had been
                   —Jeanie.

Then there came a wish
     Soft as summer streams are fresh,
To see and bear one token from thy green and early grave,
   And they pointed where the even
   Summer sunlight fell in golden shafts through clouds asunder
   ·   riven,
   On the spire that pointed upward ever, like a saint, to heaven—
Pointed to thy home above through clouds that seem'd to float and
     wave
                   —Jeanie.

     I would know the spot
     By the trees that, like a grot,
Shaded lovingly the new-made grave that held thy darling clay.
   So I bow'd in silence, keeping
   All the while a **hand upon my** breast to **keep my** heart from
     leaping
   As I whisper'd, tears were rising now, " Ah **me, so** early sleeping,
Thou that hadst **so** much **of** all that made thy **life a** summer day
                 —Jeanie."

     Then I took the path,
     Battling in my selfish wrath,
Cursing destiny, as one will curse the hand that does him **wrong;**
   But a calmer **mood** succeeded,
   Which the torture and the tumult in my restless bosom needed,
   As I climb'd the churchyard wall, and through the long, deep
     grasses speeded,
Heard the river in the distance making merry with a song
                 —Jeanie.

     This then was thy grave ;
     And my spirit, once so brave,

Wept as children will when mothers take them from their sport
   and play.
  O, they err who think a sorrow,
  By the rest of those it cherish'd, can its wonted calmness borrow.
  I stood like one who dreams and wakes to find upon the morrow
That a chaos and confusion make disorder through the day
                   —Jeanie.

       Ah me, time flew by
       As I stood thus trancedly
Gazing on the simple sod that kept so much away from me,
  Till in fancy lightly dreaming
  I beheld thee rise once more in all thy early beauty beaming ;
  But a brighter girlhood now was thine—a sweeter halo streaming
Round thy form, and awed I whisper'd—This is now the best of
     thee
                   —Jeanie.

       Happy in this thought
       I knelt down upon the spot,
Feeble with a sorrow ringing dirges through the hapless heart ;
  And I pull'd with childlike feeling
  From the grave a simple tuft of grass, and thought how all the
    reeling
  Years might come and pass, but this would still for ever be
    revealing
What no death could ever wither, so I turn'd me to depart
                  —Jeanie.

       But I linger'd still,
       As a passionate lover will
When he sees within the doorway all the centre of his love,
  Till I whisper'd—This is merely
  But the waywardness of sorrow that has worshipp'd far too
    dearly,
  But the colouring of eyes through tears that can see nothing clearly,
Grief fit only for thy smiling as thou walkest far above
                  —Jeanie.

       Now, the years that come
       Are but as shadows dumb,
Wanting all the happy order and the light they had of yore ;

Yet, betimes, when I am thinking,
And the magic past has fill'd the cup, and I am deeply drinking,
Comes the vision of a maiden, in her saintly beauty shrinking,
O, I know the face whose vanish'd sunshine beams on me no more
                    —Jeanie.

        The grass is wither'd, too,
        As all earthly things must do,
But I view it now with thoughts that make the hidden pulses
    stand.
I can feel no more the gladness
That was wont to cheer my spirit, but a double weight of sad-
    ness
Crushing down within my bosom, till I mutter, half in madness,
"There are more things wither'd than this grass I hold within my
    hand
                    —Jeanie."

———————————

THE TWILIGHT IS HERE.

THE twilight is here, and the stars are met,
    They wander side by side,
They whisper love, for their eyes are wet
    With love's own balmy tide.

I lie and watch their soft sweet looks
    As they smile in the open air ;
For their faces are sweeter to me than books,
    And many times as fair.

And I hear them whisper ever on,
    As the night its hours will spell ;
But that which they say in their whispers none
    But the wind and I can tell.

Yet if you sleep in their own sweet beams
    They will waken you up betimes
With a heart filling up with their own rich dreams
    'As mine is full of rhymes.

Therefore it comes that you catch me oft
　With my hand upon my brow,
Lying stretch'd out at length on the grass all soft,
　As you see me lying now.

And the stars look down from their place, and smile,
　And beckon, and nod, and shine ;
I seem not to heed, yet all the while
　I am making their music mine.

THE FISHERMAN.

LAUGHING eyes look over the bridge
　And seem, as they smile, to say,
　　Fisherman, have you caught to-day
Any fish ?　And I stood upon a ridge

Looking down at my line in the stream below.
　I look again, and within my heart
　　The thoughts of a past existence start,
And I live again in the long ago.

For she just so look'd in her beauty and love,
　That dear one, dead, when she spoke to me,
　　Where a Highland river is running free
Over the rocks with the sun above.

I was fishing alone by the bridge when she came,
　And such was the light on her glowing face
　　That my heart leapt up to give her a place,
And after a year she changed her name.

We were happy ; and life had the charms
　That glow in the depths of a summer sky ;
　　But a cloud rose up when none else were nigh,
And my darling wife lay dead in my arms.

Dead long ago, but still when I see
   A fair, young face looking sweetly on,
   As the fisherman steps over tree and stone,
Then I think of her that once smiled on me.

THE LONG DEEP GRASS IS SPRINGING.

THE long deep grass is springing by the edges of the streams,
  And the trees have found a secret that bursts out in leafy
     gleams ;
So to match this hour with gladness let us to the woods away,
And take with us some poet that shall teach us what to say.

Shall it be those mighty monarchs of all eloquence and ease ?
No, their songs have not the quiet that will make us love the trees ;
Keats, that only lived a summer, sung a song so full and sweet
That the gods in bounty gave him flowers for his winding sheet.

Yes, his song is wise and worthy of the stream and wood, I own,
But another is behind him with a fuller riper tone ;
Therefore let the lore of Wordsworth be our only guide to-day,
As we lie within the long deep woods and hear the branches sway.

The solemn shady forest with its gentle pulse of wind,
Is a type of all the quiet in an earnest poet's mind—
Haunting not the writhing city, but with open placid look,
Watching ever still the meadow and the sparkle of the brook.

I can fancy as I lie beneath the music of the boughs
That unseen Hamadryads wreathe the buds around their brows ;
That from the vista'd depths whose gloom the vision scarce can
     span,
Think I hear the dreamy murmurs from the drowsy pipe of Pan.

Ah, this gentle faith has pass'd away, and in the glen and wood
Sweet spirits have no more a place to fill the solitude ;
But the vision still is with us, and their beauty is a sky
That looks down upon the ages with an immortality.

Let the heart fill up with wisdom in a quiet hour like this,
Let the flowers that grow around us teach their happy mysteries.
Let the great thoughts of the mighty sweep aside the daily earth,
Till their spirits leap within us like a child before its birth ;

So that in their ampler breathing we can feel the soul outburst,
And grow into high impulses, each one wider than the first,
Till it leaps in very triumph from the daily thought of clay,
And becomes a part and being of the brightness of this day.

It is sweet to think this world, with its toil, and rush, and jar,
Cannot take this being from us, or have power to shake or mar.
Therefore, when thy heart is weary, and thy thoughts grow into pain,
Take the woods, and, in their shadows, get thy quiet back again.

THE SPIRIT OF THE WATERS.

HOW quick, and yet how soft
Comes the moonlight from aloft—
From the happy starry skies,
Like the smiles of angels' eyes,
Flinging all the silvery whiteness
Of its purity and brightness
   On the stream
That dances up with laughter
As the wavelets follow after
Each other in the glee
Of a pleasant symphony.

I stand upon the bridge,
Leaning on its narrow ledge,
Keeping watch with dreaming eye
On the river gliding by,
Till I fancy from the deeps,
Where the moonlight sits and sleeps,
I can hear a whisper say—
" Come away, come away,
Come, and never know decay,
Come, and rest beneath the stream,
And forever smile and dream.

Through the night and sunny day,
Dream of things with joyance rife,
Dream of all that makes this life
          Bright and gay.
While the waters ebb and creep
With their murmurs o'er thy sleep—
While the moonlight from above
Rains the pale wealth of her love
On the wave, on thy grave—
          Come **away**."

And I feel a strong desire
Burning in me to inquire
What this gentle sprite may be,
Who sings such **a song to** me
          From the stream.
For, **as I** hear his lay,
Like a voice from far away,
With its burden " Come away,"
I can reason thus **how sweet**
To **let** all the waters meet
O'er the weary, dreamy **head ;**
And **to** sink, as in a bed,
In the tide, **and** there to **lie**
All **the night** and watch **the** sky ;
Or sleep, **sleep,** sleep,
While the breezes come and creep—
And **what** mortal would not sleep
To such soothing lullaby,
While the happy moon above
Would fling down her wealth of **love**
On the wave, **on** my grave,
          On my dream.

WINTER VISITORS.

H, the summer time is beautiful, with all its sunny sky,
The soft sweet carol of the birds and streams that wander by ;
 But know you this, however fair, and bright, and good it be,
I would rather **have the winter,** when the dead can come to me.

I know I love the meadows, with their long sweet wealth of bloom,
And all the timid wilding flowers that find a quiet room
Within the woods, whose shadows sleep as still as aught can be;
But yet give me the winter, when the dead can come to me.

Let the fire sink into ashes as the shadows of the night
Creep upon the darken'd hearthstone in a sweet and solemn flight;
Let me bow as if in slumber, and with busy heart and brain
Try with Promethean power to start the dead to life again.

O, my heart was as a temple, where upon each incensed shrine
I had placed with all a miser's love the statues that were mine;
And I, their faithful pilgrim, paid my vows unto each one
With a more than Hindoo fervour to the cold and senseless stone.

All was gladness in this temple, as it is with those above,
And the light that I had in it was the sunshine of their love;
But death, who will not, cannot, see one mortal free from care,
Came and shook to dust and ruins all the idols I had there.

Yet within the wavy twilight, in its deepest, wisest hour,
I can act the sage magician, and can curb the churchyard's pow'r;
I can draw from out its chambers all the forms that slumber there,
Till they fill the open doorway and the dim and trembling air.

And they come and flit around me, and they sit beside my knee,
And they whisper words whose meaning none can ever know but
    me;
And so sad and sweet their language, and so faint and low they
    speak,
That I feel my bosom beating and the tears upon my cheek.

Then my heart fills up with longings as I whisper "Come once
    more,
And let each one take his chamber in my bosom as before;
Open up its rusted gateway, and from out each dusty nook
Cheer away the gloomy silence with the sunshine of your look.

O, the days are long and weary when I hear no more thy voice,
And the earth looks not the same to me, and I no more rejoice;
Come, that I may feel again the warmth of all thy vanish'd light;"
And I raise my hands to clasp them, but they vanish from my sight.

Yet they leave behind them counsels that should steer my spirit
    free
From the rocks of ill as beacons guide the mariners at sea—
Solemn counsels wisely given it were well for me to prize,
Since they point a better haven in the calm of Paradise.

Yes, the summer time is beautiful with all its clouds above,
But it brings not in the twilight all the visions that I love;
Therefore is it that I weary all the time until I see
On the hills the coming winter that will bring them back to me.

•   ————————

IN HAPPY GRANDEUR SWEPT THE MOON.

IN happy grandeur swept the moon,
   Her whispers on the silent trees,
While ever like a distant tune
   In murmurs came the breeze.

And she was with me in her life
   And beauty as the angels are,
As far apart from sin and strife
   As earth from heaven's star.

We stood, as if all human ties
   Were broken by the magic pow'r
That fell upon us from the skies
   In such a plenteous dow'r.

It seemed as if all things of light,
   And purity, and love, were near;
While we, but mortals in their sight,
   Could only stand and fear.

We stood until her fingers crept
   All tremblingly within my own;
And, looking down, I saw she wept,
   For in a tremulous tone

She whisper'd, letting droop her **head,**
　And, clasping me as if no bar
Could ever part us two, **she** said—
　" Dear love, behold **that star.**"

I turn'd me, half-inclined to fears,
　And, marking all its happy **hue,**
I whisper'd to her—" Dry thy tears,
　Its beams are **on** us two."

She spoke not, answer'd not, and now,
　When all is pass'd, and she has fled
To join the brightness of her brow
　To that one star o'erhead :

I come and gaze in silent awe
　Upon it as it glows above,
As if within its beams I saw
　The lost light of my love.

THE NIGHT IS CALM

HE night is calm, and sweet, and still—
　Such nights should ever be—
When the young and good of this earth of ours
Droop in **our** hands like wither'd flow'rs,
　To bloom in eternity.

It is **thus I** think, **as I** wander **out**
　From the dim, drear bed of death,
With longings within me of better mould,
And hopes and wishes that make **me** bold,
　And brace the **shaken** faith.

I look on the sky, **the** hill, and the stream ;
　But the only calm **I see**
Is the calm on the shrunken face of him
Asleep in the chamber wierd and dim,
　From the toil and the battle free.

Then I think if a vacant space be left
  By the dead in this heart of mine,
Let me fill it this hour with the light and love,
Coming down like a balm from the stars above—
  From a throne and a presence divine.

Alas, alas ! for the vain resolve
  That must bow before the force
Of this human grief, and the tears must rise
In a bitter flood to the weary eyes
  From my bosom's inmost source.

The stars look down from their high abodes,
    And their light is on my brow,
As they whisper—" A spirit had cross'd their way
To a brighter light than their own display,
  And was singing with angels now."

It must be so—O, this miser heart
  That will not let away
The beings we love from this worthless earth
To rise in the blush of a better birth,
  In the light of a better day.

I will weep no more, but will sit myself
  Again in the silent room,
And watch the features, childlike fair,
With their long sweet shadows gathering there,
  And bless an early tomb.

ELLEN.

ELLEN came out in the evening light
  In all her youth and love,
With a face as bright and a step as light
  As the angels are above.

The very moon in the starry skies
  Flung down a sweeter smile,

As she stood with her softly-beaming eyes
  Looking upward all the while.

Ellen ! I said, for her lips were fraught
  With the music I loved to **hear ;**
And Ellen's voice was like whispers caught
  In the night when none are near.

She spoke, and I bent to her low, sweet tone,
  That was pure as her heart within ;
And I dared **not** mingle or speak my own,
  For fear it might be sin.

But clasp **her** this night by the finger tips,
  And speak to her as you may,
Ellen will smile with thin, wan lips,
  But **not a** word will say.

GLORY.

G LORY in winning a maid in the first wild heat of our youth,
    When heaven comes down to the earth, and we walk in a
      Paradise ;
Glory in being a hero and fighting for home and for truth,
    And watch'd from a cherish'd land by a hundred thousand **eyes.**

Glory in being a statesman, with a steady **hand** on the **helm,**
    Guiding a mighty nation through **the breakers** of **courts and of
      kings** ;
Glory in fighting the hydras that struggle to overwhelm
    The liberal nature of God **in** the roll of human things.

Glory in **being** a poet, **with a** life in the eyes of the gods,
    Shaping oracular music to strike on the hearts of men ;
Glory in tracking error to the mouth of her foul abodes,
    And striking her dead with a sword in the shape of a paltry **pen.**

M 2

Glory in having the thought that can, Mentor-like, guide through
    the past,
    Probing the depths of history with swift, miraculous wand ;
That can dive into records of spleen and hate and bring out the
    truth at last,
    Like Mercury from the river with the woodman's axe in his hand.

Glory in labour, ay labour, though he hath not the gift of speech,
    He hath better in countless muscle to proffer as earth may need ;
His is the second triumph wherever his footsteps reach—
    The shock of the peopled towns and the rush of the iron steed.

These are the glories that work with men, and bud, and blossom,
    and burst,
    As the centuries roll into birth, and slowly round to their span ;
But another glory is yet to be named—the highest, the best, the
    first—
It is his who stands as a prophet speaking God's voice to man.

SONNETS.

I.

AN UNSKILLED HAND UPON THE STRINGS.

IT is a shame that I should lift my voice
  In these great days of toil, and thought, and song,
  And speak unfitting music, doing wrong
To the pure silence that should be my choice.
If song could be so curb'd. But as I stood
  By the wild steeps that guard the laurel'd hill
  A whisper came, and with a sudden thrill
Shook summer warmth through all my fleeter blood ;
Then taking voice, as evening winds will do,
  When wander'd in the grass, said, as I bent,
  "If thou hast aught of what the gods have lent,
Sing, and in singing keep thy music true."
So, with this whisper growing up, I flung
An unskilled hand upon the strings and sung.

II.

BRIGHTER THE FLOWERS.

RIGHTER the flowers still grow on him who said,
   " A thing of beauty is a joy for ever;"
     From out the past he speaks, the gentle giver
Of a mute prophecy, which on his head
Lights with an immortality that clips
   Away the earthly pathway that he trod,
   And shrines him a divinity, a god,
A spirit breathing from ethereal lips
The eloquence that we may never hear
   If we can enter not into the feeling
   That gave it birth, and hear the music stealing
Like incense upward to that timeless sphere,
Where something surer than an echo cries—
" Death is befool'd, the poet never dies."

III.

A YOUTH UPRISING

YOUTH uprising with a pale, sweet face,
  Fraught with intensest wonder, with the Muse
  For his most passionate mistress, whose rich dues
He paid with all the eloquence and grace
Of a most boyish genius, wanting only
  A few short years to ripen, and to be
  A name round which an immortality
Might wreathe its light. But Death can make all lonely
The temple of the higher gifts, and sow
  Around this life a silence. But the thought,
  The eloquence, the work can own him not.
And so he stands to us in all the glow
Of his own Endymion, a sweet breath
That speaks for ever, though all else be death.

IV.

THREE SPIRITS LINKING.

Voltaire, D'Alembert, and Diderôt.

THREE spirits linking made a triple mind,
    Then scorning customs shook the stars apart,
    And but with thought, and a most cunning art,
Shook heaven's footstool like a **sudden wind**.
Apostates from the faith of Reason, they
    Held but as food for scorn **all sacred laws**;
    Yet they fought nobly in an awful cause
(For they fight well who fight in open day).
But all in vain.   For baffled Reason fell,
    As falls a wounded bird within the night
   · Unseen, and men shook as with sudden fright,
And look'd up to the sky, but all was well,
And the mad warfare of the three but **served**
To show to unborn years where wisdom swerved.

V.

L O C H L E V E N.

WIDE lake that laps with a most liquid tongue
   The base of these worn ruins.　Have ye naught
   Within thy caverns that can aid the thought
To grasp the vanish'd years whose breath has flung
A mist o'er all I see, so that I stand
   A prey to keenest torture?　Speak, and tell
   The wonders that thy waves repictured well
When these worn ruins had strength o'er all the land.
What visions of high dames, what pages meek,
   What warriors of firm mould, what glorious **deeds,**
   What trappings of high pomp, what foaming steeds,
What chivalry of action?　Speak, O, speak,
That I may grasp the past, and open up
Its hidden feasts, and bid my being sup.

VI.

WHEREVER GENIUS WHISPERS.

WHEREVER genius whispers, " Here shall be
   An immortality for men and time
   To worship," there the ages grow sublime
And break in haloes.   Therefore unto me
   (Who make such pilgrimages in my dreams)
   Lake Leman is a mighty wish, and Rome
   A vast desire, to which all others come,
Like bubbles unto each in summer streams.
For glory is of theirs through whose wide light
   Walk those great spirits who have made this earth
   Too narrow for the effluence of that birth
Which made them all but gods.   Yet in their might
   Are they not gods, for whom we set apart
   A Grecian worship in the templed heart?

VII.

DARK EYES WITHIN WHOSE LIGHT.

DARK eyes within whose **light as** by some spell
    Girlhood and maidenhood **rise up** to claim,
By turns, a spot within their depths to dwell.
    They strive, and girlhood half retires in shame ;
Then maidenhood comes forth with modest pace,
    Laden with Iris dreams, whose **tender might**
    Tones all their glances into softer light,
And flings a sweeter shadow on the face
But for a moment—girlhood comes again
    With short, **sweet** laugh ; **and** brow, and lips, and eyes
Beam through a softly-winning smile, and then
    You start at such transition in surprise.
Thus, by sweet turns, the two still strive away,
Till rounded maidenhood **shall win the day.**

VIII.

A BLESSING ON THE TINKERS.

A BLESSING on the tinkers, and on him
   Who was their monarch—he who laid him down
   Within a prison house all damp and dim,
     And made himself immortal with his dream,
That sprung from out his heart as from the crown
     Of the sweet sky the day will come in streams
When morning breaks, and in my bosom leaps
   And frets the wish to see the quiet spot,
Where, in the calm that evil men know not,
The sacred dust of the grand dreamer sleeps,
Waiting the hour when God shall stir the dust;
     Then in all truth and humbleness will he
     Rise with his labour manifold, and be
The interpreter of his own dream and trust.

IX.

DARE I PROFANE THE WREATH ?

DARE I profane the wreath, and with blind aim
Snatch from the cunning gods who hold above
The heads of men the laurel few may love,
Since it requires a heart, and without shame
Feel its rich coolness temper **all** my brows?
Then sing, unwitting that I **held a** lyre
That echo'd only to the baser fire
Which some stray chance to meaner strings allows ;
And glowing with false hope, I strove to reach
A point of higher strength, but fell, and found
That in my own deep weakness I was bound,
Like **one** whom utter fear deprives of speech.
And in my shame I flung the wreath away,
To sing at night but never in the day.

X.

I TURN'D THE PAGES.

I TURN'D the pages writ by mighty men—
   Giants who in the past had toil'd and fought,
    And won great trophies in the war of Thought,
And with them immortality. And when
Word burst on word with all the heaven-fed glow
   Which is of genius, I stood like one
   Who hears a melody he cannot shun—
So sweet its music that perforce must grow
Upon him with its rapture. And I felt
   Another soul possess me as I caught
   The inspiration of their words ; and, fraught
With wonder at their mighty toil, I knelt,
And whisper'd with a sense of holy fear—
" They move still with us ; lo ! the Great are here."

XI.

TO BE AT YARROW.

TO be at Yarrow—this is no high wish,
  And yet what magic wraps the name. To stand
  Alone in the Parnassus of our land
With every pulse within the breast aflush
With all that song will sanctify, and slip
  Into those feelings which for ever make
  A Paradise where'er they breathe, and take
The purer utterance of the poet's lip,
And join it to the stream's whose waves still con,
  With an unalter'd eloquence, the tale
  Which is immortal, and hath lit the vale
With a most hallow'd lustre, and a tone
That speaks to all that can its spell prolong
By dreams of love and lovers and of song.

XII.

TO GO DOWN TO THE GRAVE.

O go down to the grave with many a dream
   Hid in the breast, but never clothed in words,
   With not one hope again to touch the chords
That brought such music—were but the extreme
Of a brute creed.   Far other faith than this
   Must have my worship ; for the unlaurel'd ones,
   Whose hearts were of that delicate tint which shuns
The gaze and rush of life, save that which is
Born of their fancy, after death may be
   The poets of a mightier world than ours,
   And twine each fresh burst of their spirit pow'rs
To stars and systems as they glide and flee ;
 And, safe from scorn of men and earthly things,
Shoot their ripe souls into eternal strings.

XIII.

SUCH MUSIC HAD THE GODS.

SUCH music had the gods as I have now,
 When all Olympus shook, and the quick stars
 Glimmer'd behind the golden-fretted bars
Of their dominions. At its touch the soul
Springs from its slumber, full awakenèd,
 And moves throughout the bosom with the tread
 Of some great giant. Where would be my goal,
If I should slip existence, and ascend
 With this mad music? Should I fix my home
 With the clear echoes of the sky, and roam
With all the clouds and with their colours blend?
And widen with eternity, and steal
Into infinity with all I feel?

XIV.

O, FOND ROMANCE

WHAT dreams were mine to-night, O fond romance,
  That came upon me like a summer sleep,
  And bound me so my spirit could not keep
Account with earth, but lay as in a trance
And heard Scherezadé tell again
    Her stories to the king, and saw the seas
    Brim up with pearls, golden palaces,
Slave-guarded maidens, genii on the plain,
And swarthy fishermen, and gardens rife
    With sunny fruitage—heard sweet music play
    Accompaniment to the voluptuous day—
And saw a city full of turban'd strife ;
While, as if wishing to make all complete,
The Caliph turn'd the corner of a street.

XV.

A POET IN WHOSE HEART.

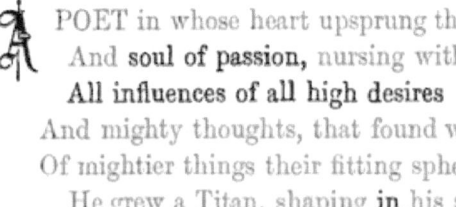 POET in whose heart upsprung the life
And **soul of passion,** nursing with its fires
All influences of all high desires
And mighty thoughts, that found within the **strife**
Of mightier things their fitting sphere. **And thus**
He grew a Titan, shaping **in** his strength
A god-like image, which became at **length**
All worn and hollow, but still luminous
With the first touch of heaven's ordaining fingers,
And giving forth those tones that hallow still
What good we **claim as ours and even ill**
(For genius consecrates where'er it **lingers),**
But Death threw down the Memnon, and its fall
Shook worlds, **and** then threw **echoes over all.**

XVI.

I KNOW NOT HOW IT IS.

KNOW not how it is, but when I hear
    The name of Wordsworth it is as a spell
    That wakes—as if the poet's self were near—
    A flood of kindred feeling.   And I dwell
With a rapt earnestness, and love, and awe
    Upon the life and spirit of him whose name
Is knit to all a placid heart can draw
    From out of Nature, and the sweet acclaim
Of all her many tones that breathe and live
For the rapt poet only.   I would give
    A lifetime's earnings if I could make mine,
In all its pure and simple healthiness,
The lore of him of Rydal, and possess
    " The vision and the faculty divine."

XVII.

SPIRIT THAT WALKEST.

SPIRIT that walkest on these waters, now
  Unseen but ever heard, take thou the form
  Most suited to thy wish, and fair and warm
Rise with a dazzling light upon thy brow,
And round thee let the dreams of those who made
  Their home by thee start up, that I may **feel**
  My inner being from its dwelling steal,
As when a beam of light strikes through the shade,
And, sinking into all thy glorious **clasp,**
  Like some wood echo when a **rest it finds,**
  I move with thee, like the invisible **winds,**
Fill'd with thy presence, and with mighty grasp
Bind all the dreams of genius into one,
And lie **within them as** within a sun.

XVIII.

A SIGH FOR THE PAST.

I LAY amid the wreck of a rude time,
  When men were rough as the huge beams they laid
  For dwellings, and within the distant shade
I saw the city sleep, and heard the chime
Of bells ; and linking, with a quiet thought,
  The mighty present to the less mighty past,
  I stood between the two, and, bowing, cast
My worship at the feet of all that sought
To place the seven-leagued boots upon advance.
  Yet could I not without regret betray
  A secret yearning for the earlier day,
When this great earth had not such wide expanse,
And men were rough, but with that roughness true
To all that pale refinement never knew.

XIX.

I WALK WITH THE STERN DANTE.

I WALK with the stern Dante through his hell :
   On either side a wall of spirits stands,
   Who **wave from out the** gloom their wailing **hands,**
And answer each with **sudden** shriek and **yell.**
I bow, not daring to look up, while fear
   Laps at my inmost soul, **as in** a lake
   The waves against a single stone will break,
And the heart, drying up, **has not one tear.**
I **sink,** half-grasping at the bard, **and he,**
   A kindred gloom upon his brow, turns round ;
   When, lo, a spirit from the gloomy **bound**
Glides in between the Florentine and me,
Who, as he feels his skirt, cries in dismay,
Qual maraviglia, and I swoon away.

XX.

IT WAS A SPOT SO QUIET.

IT was a spot so quiet that the stream
  Was in itself a silence, and the wood
   Slept as if Somnus in a dreary mood
Had wept down tears upon it from the beam
Of his sleep-wearied eyes; and far away,
  Through a long vista of deep shade, was seen
   A little spot of soft and brightest green,
Whereon the moonlight, sister to the day,
Was feasting. In such spot as this the wise
Might come and break the twining snake-like thralls
  Of hydra'd error, or great Pan himself
Come forth and hear the shepherds sacrifice,
  Or Oberon, sweet king of fairy elf,
Lead forth his queen in midnight festivals.

www.ingramcontent.com/pod-product-compliance
Lightning Source LLC
Chambersburg PA
CBHW020617030726
47497CB00007B/2294